THE URBANA FREE LIBRARY
W9-BCD-278

Simone

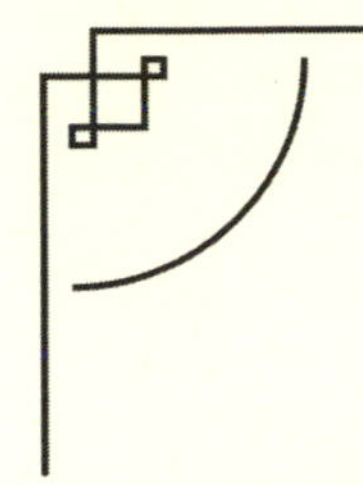
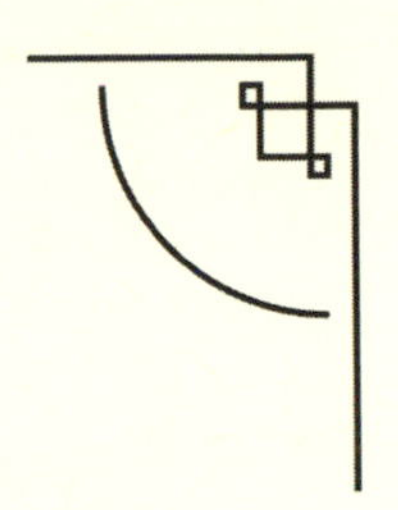

Simone

A Novel

EDUARDO LALO

Translated by David Frye

THE UNIVERSITY OF CHICAGO PRESS
CHICAGO AND LONDON

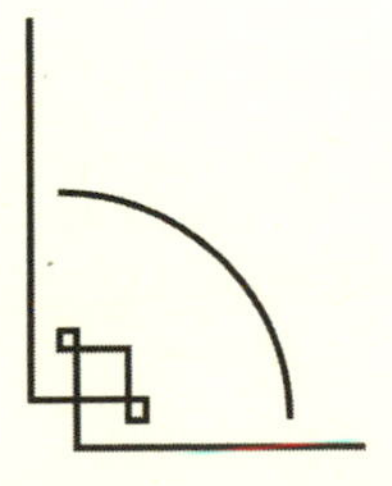
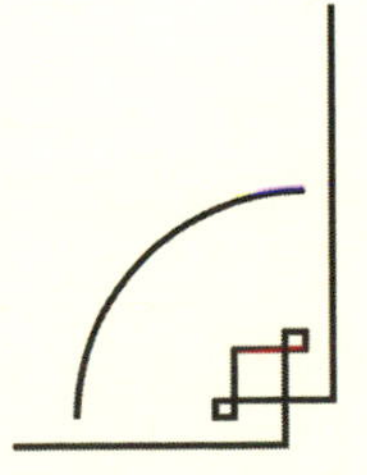

EDUARDO LALO *is a writer, essayist, video artist, and photographer from Puerto Rico. He is the author of ten Spanish-language books, including* La Inutilidad, Los Países Invisibles, *and, most recently,* El Deseo del Lápiz.

DAVID FRYE *is a lecturer in anthropology at the University of Michigan who translates both Spanish poetry and prose.*

The University of Chicago Press, Chicago 60637

Printed in the United States of America

24 23 22 21 20 19 18 17 16 15   1 2 3 4 5

ISBN-13: 978-0-226-20748-3 (paper)
ISBN-13: 978-0-226-20751-3 (e-book)
DOI: 10.7208/chicago/9780226207513.001.0001

Published by arrangement with Ediciones Corregidor S.A.I.C.y E.,
Buenos Aires, Argentina.

Library of Congress Cataloging-in-Publication Data

Lalo, Eduardo, 1960– author.
[Simone. English]
Simone : a novel / Eduardo Lalo ; translated by David Frye.
pages ; cm
ISBN 978-0-226-20748-3 (pbk. : alk. paper) — ISBN 978-0-226-20751-3 (ebook)
1. Authors, Spanish—Puerto Rico—San Juan—Fiction. I. Frye, David L., translator. II. Title.
PQ7440.L29S5613 2015
863'.64—dc23
2015010766

♾ This paper meets the requirements of ANSI/NISO Z39.48-1992 (Permanence of Paper).

to **Grisell**

. . . il n'est pas de désir plus grand que celui
du blessé pour une autre blessure.

. . . No greater desire exists than a wounded
person's need for another wound.

Georges Bataille, LE COUPABLE

• • •

Habla con su propia palabra sólo la herida.

Only the wound speaks its own word.

Antonio Porchia, VOCES

Simone

Writing. What other choice do I have in this world, where so many things are forever beyond my reach? But I'm still here, alive and irrepressible, and it doesn't matter if I've been condemned to corners, to cupboards, to nothingness.

Thoughts emerging from out of nowhere, from the "nothing's happening," from the here and now. I say this with the joy you feel when you've lost all hope yet still persist, still survive. Writing with no exit, from anywhere. In this opaque city, for instance, where I know my neighbors can't understand why I'm writing and, in any case, they won't ever see these pages. Writing from a dead end that will always remain a dead end that may have never been anything else. So many men and women have believed in the possibility of changing history, yet all they ever did was suffer it. Or maybe I should say: all they did was put up with their neighbors, their family, their wives, themselves. I've taken the blows and I'm still standing. That's about all I've accomplished. That is what writing or reading is good for, and I've devoted nearly my whole life to it. Now and then, I've known something akin to grace.

Another Sunday morning. The quiet street, a few kids shouting, a brief gust of wind swirling leaves down the sidewalk. The restless day of rest. Blessed are the birds that sing today like any other day—that is, without hope.

Most of what's called depression consists of store-bought feelings. I call them that for good reason: I'm speaking from experience. Our emotions pop off the assembly line, you can pick them up anywhere. There's a mass distribution network. Like so many other things we buy and sell, they're cheap knockoffs. They exist because we adopt specific ways of being and feeling to face specific events. That's about all.

But sometimes your depression stirs up no feelings, so it hardly deserves the name. It's just what's left when time's up and so many things have been lost or will never be gained, and you know there's nothing to hope for in the end but this: this Sunday morning.

That may sound stark, but I find it comforting to think this way.

A journal. This notebook, the umpteenth in my lifetime, bought at a nondescript bookstore in an equally nondescript shopping center (leaving a bookstore with only a tome of blank pages is a metaphor, but also a form of grief and boredom). Its paper is surprisingly good, though the notebook itself turns out to be a little thick for resting my hand on while writing this. I'm using these pages to log the passage of time. I want the notebook to be a tool for living as best I can, for making it through the day, through the year, while preserving some scrap of sanity and pleasure. Before, in my older journals—now tucked away in corners and bookshelves at home—I used to think I was struggling against the society I was forced to live in. Against this city. Against the unbearable succession of classrooms where I'd made my living until I landed a steady job (though my contract could be revoked at the end of any semester) at the university. (And I felt ashamed of that struggle, as if there were something disgracefully dirty and paltry about it.) But now I know that struggling and writing are the same thing, whether there's anything to write or struggle against. I'm not expecting anything major, no truce, no triumph. This is my place in the world, that's all.

Diego told me it was only after he was able to move far from San Juan that he came to know beauty. He didn't mean beautiful landscapes or beautiful bodies. He was already a young man by the time he managed to leave our country, Puerto Rico. Only then did he fully grasp how much misery he'd lived through. He remembered years spent in the schoolyard, surrounded by screeching schoolmates, under the midday sun, in the thick, dry clouds of dust they raised as they ran about. He obsessively recalled his teachers' fruitless goodwill, the mounting pressure during class time, and the curriculum that made him despise for years the things he was forced to learn. And then, as if in a never-ending story, came the bell freeing him for the rest of the day, the stampede of kids shoving toward the water fountain, the games that kept getting more and more vicious, the interminable wait for the bus. Then arriving one hour later, dirty and exhausted, at his house in a city that has no prospects, nothing for a teenage boy to do but roam aimlessly and throw rocks at lamp posts, at neighbors' houses, at lizards, at the kids on the next block. Diego used to say, with all his fury still smoldering in his words, that it took him more than twenty years to realize that such a thing as beauty existed, that it could be found in a shrug, in a glance, in a leap, in a book. Though he'd had the good luck of discovering it, a gift in itself, he had never managed to free himself from that schoolyard, those teachers, those schoolmates and rivals. He was stuck with them for good, and he discovered, as a full-grown man, that he was a loser. That's all the good discovering beauty did him.

In my afternoon snooze, I had the dream again. I'm underground in an open space from which, after a whole series of apparently unconnected scenes, I am struggling to extract myself. This time, I had to climb a vast incline inside what looked like a metro station or the old lobby of the boarding lounge at the San Juan airport. But I couldn't do it, it was too hard, and my feet seemed glued to the floor. I kept looking back (as I always do in this dream), trying to communicate with another person (almost always a woman), but I couldn't find her, or my voice wouldn't reach her.

It's odd, this underground trap I can never leave. Apparently, there's some country that I find myself unable to depart from; travel and connections with other human beings are impossible. The fact that it takes place underground—in a tomb or a trap—makes the point so obvious that it borders on the redundant. The space is lit exactly like a shopping mall. It is, then, a cave made from the most ignoble of materials. Isn't the impossibility of escaping this space an image of me in this city?

It took such a short stretch of time, watching the news on Televisión Española, to encapsulate what had taken me a long time to live. The news program ended with their announcement of an upcoming concert by a singer celebrating sixteen years of performing solo. I watched his skeletal figure for thirty seconds, until the credits rolled. He wore a jacket (but not the sort an executive or a salesman would wear) and moved his head away from the microphone to take a deep breath before each verse. Years and excesses had taken their toll in equally brutal measure.

If I'd stayed in Madrid, I would have recognized him. All the same, I was convinced as I heard him sing that, even if I had remained there, I could never have made that world my own or become a part of the generation I'd been born into. I was too intensely discontented back then. There was no place—and no concert—where I would have belonged. This distance from everything around me, nearly the same as I'd later feel in San Juan, already stood between the person I was and the world. Geography and travel were infinitely less real than my feeling alone.

I don't buy newspapers. Lately I've started to get them again on occasion; the wealth of absurdities in them amuses me. Yesterday I ripped half a page from *Primera Hora* and stuck it in my back pocket. Today I found it. In a column listing the opinions of people that the reporter interviewed on the street, six citizens were asked whether they thought the war in Iraq, which seems to be right around the corner, will go on for very long.

The first man, whose impossible name was Hovitt Plancdeball, stated, "I don't think it will last long. Because of all the technological advances, that won't be necessary. They'll drop a bomb and that's it, it won't even be like the Gulf War."

A woman addressed the question: "Not long, I don't think. With all that technology, they'll definitely finish quick and start a dialogue because, otherwise, it could lead to worse consequences." Curious, this notion that dialogue could only begin after bombardment (discussing, I imagine, various ways to surrender) and that the absence of such a dialogue could forebode something worse.

A man said, "Short. Our technology" (*our*?) "is much more advanced, and the American people would never agree to that." (*That*? What is *that*?) "They'd start putting yellow signs" (shouldn't it be yellow *ribbons*?) "up everywhere."

There's only one dissident voice: "Plenty, a lot longer than they think. I pray to God that it won't cause too much devastation and that it will end as soon as possible."

But my favorite opinion comes from an advertising agent from Carolina—young and attractive, to judge by her photo; an idiot, to judge by the rest: "Short. We aren't living in the old days anymore." (Apparently in the past everything was worse.) "We're a little lighter on our feet now and people have to have more civilization and resolve things faster." This way of looking at war is extraordinary, like love advice or an offer from a telemarketer.

—The new arrivals are on the table.
—Yeah, I saw.
—We just got García Márquez's new novel.
—Not interested.

I see a bumper sticker. It says, "I am a citizen of Heaven." Ironically, the phrase floats above twinned flags of Puerto Rico and the

United States. Below it there's a Bible quote and the names of a pastor and a church, but the lettering is too small for me to read.

Get up, see and hear the city. Think: I've wasted my life here and now it's too late. Think: it would have been the same anywhere else, but it doesn't matter, I would have preferred anywhere else.

Outside, the loudspeakers blaring from a politician's campaign car promise fireworks and "surprises" in front of campaign headquarters tonight after five.

Today everything is too painful, and yet I am nearly at peace. It's because pain has become a habit. I no longer notice the incessant hum.

I spend Sunday afternoon correcting exams. One student has written, "The Renaissance started when people realized it wasn't the Middle Ages anymore."

Diego, who has been frequenting the airport for some time now, told me about him. The man is retired. As a boy, he lived in New York, and after he returned to Puerto Rico, he left rarely and for short trips. It's been years now since he's boarded a plane. Every week he spends at least one night at the international airport. He strides along the wide concourses like just another passenger. He shows up at the food stands, reads the newspaper or a novel as if he were killing time on a long layover, sits at a bar near the boarding gates. He buys knickknacks, magazines, and countless best sellers in those all-night stores.

Sometimes, suffering from insomnia, he goes to the airport in the small hours of the morning, when it's practically deserted and the workers are polishing the floors with machines. He walks through both levels, arrivals and departures, along the outdoor sidewalks that were crowded with people all day and half the night and where now you might see nothing passing by but a taxi or a service truck.

Out there, he feels the night breeze, stares at the black spots on the cement (old chewing gum stains), reads the signs at the post office or customs booth announcing hours, holidays, and obscure laws. He stops walking when he feels a vibration growing until it turns into a takeoff or landing. He attends the thundering din, much as others sip coffee or savor a dessert. Then, nodding off in a chair, greeting through his yawns the cleaning crews or airline workers he's met, he waits for the shops to open. He has a couple of eggs for breakfast at a cafeteria, and before leaving, he buys the newspaper and sometimes a *National Geographic*. He goes home while hundreds of people are rushing along the highways in the other direction to catch their morning fights.

I've been very impressed by the adventures of this man who inhabits the borders of travel indefinitely, as if they would exhaust his desire to leave. Few people travel so often, so slowly, so close to home.

A curious phenomenon: if I don't jot down a memory or an idea, it loses all its power, as if the substance of the thought had dried up, leaving it forever inert. It's as if I could only discern life through ink.

I walk toward four young women and from a distance I perceive the aura of stupidity. As they pass me, I hear one saying, "Addy is famous among the world of the homosexuals." The sentence doesn't hold together, not only because of the misused preposition. She pronounces the last word clumsily, partly swallowing the sound of the *m*, as if it were too big for her mouth.

A student hands me a note, signed with only her first name: Cindidet. We both live in the same city. Nevertheless, this absurd, made-up name seems to open an unbridgeable distance between us.

I think about all the times I've read or written the concept, "Puerto Rico." Thousands, perhaps tens of thousands of times, and yet those words are hardly ever written or read anywhere but here. What's more, they are practically unknown, or they suggest very weak images having little to do with what they mean to me. This is something I think whenever I read, write, hear this name of a country that means so little beyond its borders (and perhaps within them, too). What sort of silence is this? That is to say, what sort of pain?

Somewhere in the city (I know I saw it with Diego years ago), there's a coffee shop called "Our Daily Bread." Unbelievable, such a pious tautology. Is it in Barrio Obrero, Villa Palmeras, or on a street around Avenida Fernández Juncos? I don't know, and this incomplete memory is also a part of San Juan.

Late last night, I went to get takeout from a Chinese restaurant near Avenida Barbosa. I'd never gone in there, and I felt nervous stepping out of the car. The atmosphere was tense: a couple of drug addicts out begging, shady teenagers keeping an eye on everyone who approached, men drinking beer and shouting under the corner streetlight.

When they handed me my food, a man came in who said hello to the fellow behind me in line. Then the guard at the door, apparently an indispensable employee around there, went up to him:

"You left your engine running."

"Yeah, if I turn it off I have to push-start it."

When I left, carrying my order of fried rice in a bag, I spotted the old Yamaha. In terrible condition, its motor chugging. Not even worth stealing.

I've reread *The Stranger* after many years, focusing on Camus's use of the sun. Meursault, the protagonist, authentically perceives things the way someone suffering from too much sun would, someone who'd even kill because of it. His is not the tourists' sun; there's no paradise here. His sun is simply what one has to endure day after day, week after week, month after month, year after year. It heightens poverty, despondency, the neighbors' shouting.

Curiosity aroused, I found the only text I have about Camus. I opened it at random and started reading a paragraph: "Due to his health, he was forced to leave the Algerian summer. Camus obtained a safe-conduct pass to return, with his wife, to the mother country." Was he another victim of the sun? Could the sun be a sort of illness that for centuries has been producing the sensation that life is unlivable?

I picture myself here, sitting alone at this table in a shopping center courtyard food court, with my coffee and notebook. At my feet, a backpack with books, another notebook, and two fountain pens. I've been here for hours and haven't bought anything, not even a book. It's incredibly odd, given everything around me, but I find no other image so haunting and disturbing.

"Even in our own day, nine-tenths of humanity is outside history, outside a system of interpretation and recording which was born with modern times and will disappear. History is a kind of luxury Western societies have afforded themselves. It's 'their' history. The fact that it seems to be disappearing is unfortunate for us, but it allows destiny, which has always been the lot of other cultures, to take over. The other cultures have never lacked destiny, whereas we, in our Western societies, are bereft of it." Jean Baudrillard, *Le Paroxyste indifférent*.

I dreamed of Tomás and his wife. I should have seen him yesterday but I didn't go to work. I like talking to him, but sometimes we have a hard time in spite of all our shared interests, including books. In the dream, his image returned over and over again. We spoke briefly and unintelligibly, and we kept having to separate and then talk again, as if the whole thing were a long, drawn-out, missed connection.

I saw him looking at me, and it took me a few seconds to recognize him. I almost got to the point where my reaction would have been too late. Two or three years ago, or maybe a little more, he worked with me for a brief period. A young man, quiet, superficially coarse. I later learned that he had been on death's doorstep. When I went up to him, I couldn't remember his name, but I did remember his condition and that's what we talked about. His situation has improved, but as he told me about it, I could tell he was deeply exhausted. I gave him the banal support that a stranger might offer. When he said good-bye, I noticed that he shaved his forearms, the way bodybuilders do, and I was simultaneously impressed by how lightly he shook my hand. As if he doubted my presence.

I discover the name of a woman who works in an art supply store: Arles Pages. *Arles*, like the city that van Gogh made famous and the well-known brand of pricey watercolor drawing paper. *Pages*, as in pieces of paper in English or French. Her name is like one of the products she sells. She hadn't noticed. She didn't care to know.

I'm watching a red-tailed hawk, a *guaraguao*, from the café at the Borders bookstore in Plaza Escorial in Carolina. It glides skillfully above the housing development behind the shopping center, where a wooded hill still survives. I remember the stories I sometimes told my friends' children, in which these birds were the protagonists; how they felt a longing for their lost world, a nostalgia that could degenerate into sentimentalism.

Next to me a Chinese man is thumbing through a volume in a series of popular novels titled *Predator*. His daughter, sitting across from him, is no more than three, but he's given her his coffee to taste. They had spoken in Chinese earlier, but when she puts her lips to the coffee cup, the little girl wrinkles her nose and says "Fo!" like any Puerto Rican. There must be thousands of Chinese people in the country (just count everyone working in restaurants), but they're invisible. I've sometimes wonder what their lives must be like, how they've ended up here, how they feel.

Is anyone counting us, the people living on this island? Do we exist for anyone, on this secretive afternoon, as we try to detach from the noise, the heat, the dust? Who hears our life stories? Are we known anywhere by anything other than clichés about us or vague, simplistic accounts of us that deny us our humanity?

A man is pushing his coconut and pineapple ice-cream cart along the sidewalk of Avenida Ponce de León, near the university. He's wearing a pair of very cheap, worn-out sneakers, laces untied, like the ones they sell at a shoe store in the Plaza del Mercado in Río Piedras. He's walking very slowly, hawking his wares unenthusiastically, as if by this time in the afternoon he doesn't really care.

"The guilty feelings of those who write are well known, and they partly explain our obsession with putting the pen at the service of 'worthy causes' in order to feel less useless." Gabriel Zaid, *So Many Books*.

I'm reading Zaid in a coffee shop. Near me, three Cubans are shouting more than talking to each other. The youngest, with a fantastically carved walking cane resting between his legs, says he didn't see a cow until he was seventeen years old.

The improbable conversation distracts me. Zaid analyzes the act of reading, from learning how to spell out words to the comprehension of a book as a whole. "People who feel this way don't read books. They never really learned to read books. Reading never appealed to them. They never acquired a taste for reading, and so they will never enjoy it." I'm thinking about these men with their booming voices, meant to raise the value of what they're saying, about the coffee shop workers, about the other people eating here. I'm the only one in the whole place with a book. At this hour, already well into the morning, nobody even has a newspaper. When I sat down and pulled the book out of my backpack, I felt a slight, distant sense of shame. As if I were making a fool of myself in the schoolyard.

I note with relief that the Cubans have stood up and are going to pay. An old Puerto Rican, who stands by the cash register in hopes of getting a coffee, has heard them and interrupts the one with the cane:

—And when you saw the cow, did you think it was a kangaroo?

The Cuban is sickly thin and wears false teeth. He doesn't like it when others butt into his business, and in answer, he makes an unclear gesture meant to settle the matter. But the old man, who has just gotten his coffee, keeps up the joke:

—Where were you living? In New York?

In the geographic and conceptual choices behind his questions lies a lot of history and a whole limited view of the world. Apparently the Cuban feels that he has to establish a distinction.

—No, he answers. In a city where there weren't any cows.

He says it with arrogant pride. His answer, I know, is imbued with a mythic concept of Havana as progress and modernity held back by history.

I reach the last page of a chapter in *So Many Books*: "Reading is not the act of spelling out words, or the effort of dragging oneself across the surface of a mural that will never be viewed in its entirety. Beyond the alphabet, the paragraph, and the short article which may still be taken in all at once, there are functional illiteracies of the book. The great barrier to the free circulation of books is the mass of privileged citizens who have college degrees but never learned to read properly . . ."

The Cubans finally leave and the door is about to close when the old man exclaims:

—Guess what, I lived next to a slaughterhouse! Didn't I see cows!

It is amazing what happens without anything happening. Here I am, sitting in front of a cup of coffee, reading a book, writing in a notebook.

"The human race publishes a book every thirty seconds." Gabriel Zaid, *So Many Books*.

Diego, who's been living abroad for longer and longer periods since he started working at the bank, has begun to neglect me, like so many other aspects of his past. I've seen this happen to plenty of people but never thought I'd see it with him. He must think his chance to leave the country came too late in life, and the years of stultifying frustration are now manifesting as disdain. Just like me, he was too eager, but I left at a much younger age and the moment came when I knew I had to return, even if I didn't really know what I was coming back to. I don't judge him, but this is the first time anything's come between us since we've known each other. This break between us is a kind of violence. Nobody deserves it. A reminder that this society hardly even counts for him anymore, yet he can't get away from it.

A young, attractive woman, walking with her two children. She's dressed simply (jeans, blouse) and wearing heavy makeup. She buys snacks for the three of them but ends up eating everything herself, except for a couple of bites her older son nibbles. She talks to the clerk at the coffee shop and to someone on her cell phone with a naturalness that seems affected and puts me off. You could say she seems like a foreigner; here that would be taken as a compliment. She allows the boys to run around, doesn't shout at them, does everything at a slow pace, so comfortable at it that it's almost insulting. She doesn't mind being watched. We all know she's rich and couldn't care less what we think.

When she leaves, the memory of her still bothers me. I can't help this feeling of oppression, which comes from way back. A whole history of humiliations I've never been able to pin down.

"It pained me that on the streets of the city where I had lived most of my life nothing should be happening. It was like any other place in the world, people were born, grew up, suffered, fell in love, survived, died, the whole comedy and the whole tragedy, but at the same time and over the long run, here nothing ever happened. Nothing that I or people like me could do would create more than passing waves in a pond. Our place in history, our efforts to live and leave a mark, a narrative, were not permitted to exist. We claimed to be a country, but in reality even many of those who were convinced of that fact acted as if we were nothing but a stop on an empire's bus route. We barely had words, only gestures, maybe a few ways of destroying ourselves. A shopkeeper could be at peace any place. Money worked just as it did anywhere else. But all I had were words that would never be heard or read; terms from an unknown city that was scarcely real even to its own inhabitants."

This is a paragraph by Máximo Noreña. I've read it so many times I've practically learned it by heart. It expresses the agony of generations of people and reading it gives me, ironically, a sense of peace. A desperate peace, to be sure, but ultimately peace, as if I suspected that something had happened in the city because someone had been capable of writing this paragraph.

"To what degree can we build a society based on lies and forgetting?"

At the exit to the university building, this was written in chalk on the sidewalk. I didn't think it could have anything to do with me. It sounded like a slogan, a protest aimed at everyone and at no one. The next messages quickly made me change my mind.

I'd never seen a public statement written like that, in chalk, so willingly ephemeral. Political declarations tended to go for the aggressive hostility of paint. The block letters were almost childish and leaned to the right. At that moment I read it without suspecting it might have something to do with me.

A few days later I found a small, wrinkled piece of paper (barely a quarter of a sheet of notebook paper) that someone had slipped under the door to my office.

MONDAY, 8:1?.

I am Lina, the blond, pale-skinned, short-haired, blue-eyed girl who wrote on the street, 'To what degree can we build a society based on lies and forgetting?' I came looking for you, but I don't want to find you. I want you to read me. I'll be back on Wednesday at around 12:xx. I hope to be able to see you without our needing to talk. I prefer for you to read me and for me to read you. Thank you for your attention and sincerity.

Seriously,

Simone

I remember the early eighties, when I lived in old San Juan. At night I'd see how the ships (cruise ships, freighters, yachts) entered the bay wrapped in an unreal silence. It was new to me and completely magical. Never before had I lived near a port, neither here nor abroad. The traffic of great ships intensified the flavor of city living and taught me something obvious yet oddly difficult to believe: San Juan could be a destination, a point of arrival for sailors and vessels that I imagined coming from countries all over the world.

The sirens wailing at the mouth of the bay were the most comforting sound that, up to then, I had ever heard.

The day I wrote this, an unsealed white envelope appeared in my mail box at the university. It contained two sheets of paper covered with large and irregular block letters, spelling out what looked like an unidentified quotation:

> As expected, I have remained in Manchester to this day, Ferber continued. It is now twenty-two years since I arrived, he said, and with every year that passes a change of place seems less conceivable. Manchester has taken possession of me for good. I cannot leave, I do not want to leave, I must not. Even the visits I have to make

to London once or twice a year oppress and upset me. Waiting at the stations, the announcements over the public address, sitting on the train, the countryside passing by (which is still quite unknown to me), the looks of the fellow passengers—all of it is torture to me. That is why I have rarely been anywhere in my life, except of course Manchester; and even here I often don't leave the house or workshop for weeks on end.

In Río Piedras two women are talking on the street:

—I want to be blonder.

—But you, your hair is so nice and fine, and it's so easy to dye.

I know what they are saying, but in reality, what are they saying? How are words possible for something I do not wish to understand?

I dreamed of an area in the center of the island that doesn't exist. Very mountainous (with peaks much higher than the ones in the Cordillera Central) and tall cliffs of sheer rock with no vegetation. In one place there's a waterfall, and then a photo. In the photo, I'm very thin and have long hair, parted the way I wore it when I started at the university. Behind me is my partner during that moment beyond time. A thin, foreign woman (probably North American) who smiles at me with a great deal of affection. Something suggests that we met and fell in love while working together on whatever it was that brought her to the country. However, she will be leaving soon, and in the dream, there's a sense of a couple of letters. Distance will not allow this romance to continue. What's left is this photo, suggesting nostalgia for the impossible, for these cliffs and mountains that are somehow associated with us. The cruel certainty of dreams, telling me that this woman whom I am losing forever has been a part of my life story.

I think of the women I've been involved with, each relationship ending in disappointment. In the end, it always devolved into

Department of Kinesiology and Community Health

I have been invited to Freer Hall today to participate in a research project.

Please do not tow my car.

Date: 3/4/16

Research Project: COMPARE

EPL-[illegible]

tallying losses, into tiresome negotiations to create a barely livable situation: company, sex, conversations, a soft and capricious tenderness. I put up with what almost always struck me as their narrow-mindedness: the ridiculous obsessions, the dreams of weddings and progeny, the search for an apartment we couldn't afford in El Condado. We were always victims of the long, slow dissolution of what was never fully there.

Followed by our haphazard, widely spaced encounters in the street, perfect for acting out, certain we could always retreat. My survival strategies: a stupid desire to live in any hole in the wall, a tremendous craving for a smoke, a yearning to lose myself in a solitude that was both a chrysalis and an offensive weapon, my useless disappearance, and my useless violence.

I've always been just as I've described myself here: surrounded by fragments, by bits of things with which to fill the hours.

I've learned to live amid the rubble, satisfied not to be satisfied, supposing these circumstances link me to a multitude of men and women whom I will make no effort to meet, but with whom I feel a sort of kinship much more powerful than I've had with most of the people I actually know. This is how I've lived, with no possibility of a reasonable excuse. I've become a creature of habit and run out of arguments. I try to explain why I still feel shreds of something like a childish sense of shame, but my shame too has lost ground. I explain without a reason now. Free.

My e-mail inbox received a message that seems to consist exclusively of one quote:

"As he watched the small towns and lonely mines go by, he ran into reminders of his past that transported him to the rest of the world. . . . For a dead man, the whole world was a giant funeral."

The sender's unlikely e-mail address belonged to a beauty academy.

The world of the future (the future?): people wandering through the streets, the plaza, the highways, the stages of life, *without understanding any of it*.

That time when, arriving at the airport in New York, I pretended to be a Paraguayan, and I told the woman who shared the taxi with me (a US citizen, over the age of fifty, married to a lawyer with a degree from Columbia University) that I had been on a trip with many layovers all across South America. It wasn't that saying I was coming from Puerto Rico seemed like too little to me. My struggle was to keep her from attributing one of the few images she had at hand to me. My humanity didn't fit them, and it rebelled. But why did I pretend to be a Paraguayan, which for her was even harder to place, less real? Why emphasize the distance, the length, complexity, and phantom nature of the trip? What was I telling her? Why was I in such a rush to impose a distance between us that put practically everything off limits?

Another message has appeared in my inbox: "Struggles have become all but incommunicable." Could it be from Lina? Or from Simone? The sentence forms a solid column in which it is repeated at least fifty times. At the end, after a blank line, it says, "For you. Is it you?"

It was impossible to know how he, or she, got my address. Obviously the game was afoot. I was in the sights of a sharpshooter who wanted to toy with me.

I must admit that I like getting the messages. More than a week has gone by since the last one. Are they original texts or quotations? And I fantasize that the writer might be a woman.

On the street, I find myself watching my back. I'm not afraid of anything, but I think I can detect eyes spying on me.

I also consider the fact that these messages, which seem to arrive on sunbeams or on the wind, could surely only happen here, that they're a form that life takes on in San Juan. Like this, like writing at this table with a tangle of feelings lashing out against the ocean that separates us from everything and everybody, even our friends, such as Diego. For some reason we've chosen to talk without looking at ourselves, without knowing for sure who we are, without any real contact. The routine of the city: solitude drives down the highways, making pit stops at twenty-four-hour gas stations.

I'm in the Iberia coffee shop on Avenida Ponce de León. It's Saturday and the afternoon is beginning. There's hardly anyone here. A waitress with dyed blond hair and an incredibly childish voice sweeps the floor. In the far corner, an old couple talks in low whispers. The man is from the United States and has ordered two *café con leches* in his heavy accent. A TV set mounted near the ceiling is blaring. No one watches it.

Through the storefront window, I see it's drizzling, as it's been for the past two days. The city of insufferable sun has its indoor days. A Saturday, traffic is light and flows easily. Across the street there used to be an appliance store where I'd go with my parents more than twenty years ago. I bought a refrigerator there myself, for one of my first apartments. I remember that in this coffee shop, more than a decade ago, I tried to buy a sandwich one wretched night when the whole city was celebrating, because they were setting off fireworks in honor of the Quincentennial.

Here I am, waiting for the next message, already aware that I find something in them that I don't have in myself and that I desire. What is it? Who am I, what do I represent to that other person? What are they looking for, to go to such lengths?

Yesterday, at the stoplight where Avenida Ponce de León meets Roosevelt, the addict I see every day and to whom I haven't given a penny in months knocked on the car window and showed me an envelope with my name written in block letters. I opened the window. "It's for you, mister. How are you today?" "OK, you?" It's conventional to treat the poor brusquely, so it would have been a mockery to return his formality. "As you find me, mister," he replied. "See you," I said when the traffic started up again, convinced that in the future he would start to form part of my small circle of relations.

I managed to open the envelope, which was heavily sealed with tape, while shifting gears and changing lanes, but even so, I didn't manage to keep my fellow drivers from honking their horns at me. I turned onto a street in Hato Rey and looked for a place to park in the working-class neighborhood that's still there, a block from the pomp of the banking district. In front of an auto shop, I found a driveway where I could pull off of the street, and I unfolded the paper. "When I asked if he remembered saying good-bye to his parents in the airport, he replied, after a long hesitation, that when he thought back to that May morning at Oberwiesenfeld he could not see his parents. He no longer knew what the last thing his mother or father had said to him was, or he to them, or whether his parents had embraced or not."

The message was as heartbreaking as the crudely handwritten phrase that the shop owner, no doubt a former drug addict converted to Evangelical Christianity, had posted over the entrance: "Drugs kill." Now I saw him eyeing me from inside the shop, perturbed by my indecisively parked car, standing in a shop entrance papered with two or three months' worth of centerfolds of women in bikinis from copies of *Primera Hora*. Curious combination of Christ Jesus and the finest tits the country has to offer.

I backed up and drove back to the avenue. Tried not to think. It was preferable, for now, to savor both the pleasure and the uncertainty.

It had been a couple of years since a publisher brought my first three books back into print in a volume called *Three-in-One*. I loved the play on words. "Three-in-One" was a brand of oil I used as a child to lubricate my bicycle. My books, which had suffered from neglect and editorial ineptitude, had returned to the land of the living (or of the reading) with relative success. They were circulating by dribs and drabs, but I knew that normally things were much worse. I had been impressed when the woman at an ice cream parlor in El Condado, instead of taking my order, asked me about the plot of a novel and scooped the vanilla ice cream while enthusiastically describing how she read it or when a secretary in a doctor's office who read my name on a form asked me if I was the writer of the same name and proceeded to interrogate me until the coughs of waiting patients forced her to end her impromptu interview.

These literary encounters, which took place on a number of occasions, were new to me. I had gotten used to writing for nobody because in my case the cliché of writing for your friends didn't fit. My friends (with the partial exception of Diego because not even he had read everything) and my girlfriends weren't particularly interested in my writing. So over the years, without getting metaphorical about it, I had resigned myself to writing for nobody, or rather, for my hand: writing gave me something to do with it, something to do with my life. Probably the reason I didn't quit was that in my final years of high school, and later at the university, this was the identity I wanted to give myself because I revered book cover photos, not posters of actors or athletes; because in the end, despite the scale of the effort and the thankless indifference, what meant the most to me, even more than women, were books.

So it was natural for me to suppose that the mysterious message writer was inspired by an enthusiastic reading of my work. Something had to have motivated this person to seek me out because the notes I was given, or the phrases written in chalk or sent by e-mail, were, in addition to attempts at seduction, a proof of literary passion.

Julia phoned, and as we talked, it occurred to me she might be the one sending messages. We'd been partners. She knew my tastes, where I worked. Thinking it over, I lost track of the conversation. "Are you there? Still listening?" I could hear her annoyance. Her tone convinced me it couldn't be her. She almost wanted me to listen to her by force, wanted me to love her. I was sure that under other circumstances we'd rather not be talking at all, or even to have ever met. Besides, she wasn't patient or subtle enough for those messages. No, it couldn't be Julia. Or rather, I thought, it *shouldn't* be Julia.

I like writing on the backs of flyers that people hand me on the street. My notes go on advertising leaflets and also on receipts. Now, for example, I'm writing on the back of an ad for a company that does roof repair and similar services. I first read the message from the company, which, like so many others here, has a pompous English name under which it lists its services in everyday Spanish.

I write anywhere. Ink flows like magic across cheap paper.

"The Center for Academic Excellence invites you to our 'Workshop on the Comma' and our 'Workshop on Pronouns and Adverbs; Prepositions and Conjunctions.' These two workshops will be conducted by our resident professors of linguistic competence in the vernacular and are requirements for the Institute for Composition in the Vernacular."

Is there anything to add, in the vernacular?

In what is now a familiarly disconcerting ritual, two days after the last note (on Saturday; today is Monday), I found an envelope in my home mailbox. From the San Juan Biennial of Latin American and Caribbean Printmaking, according to the return address, it was an invitation to take part in the Eleventh International Biennial Print and Drawing Exhibition in Taipei. A form letter photocopied to be distributed to a long list of addressees, no doubt. It was odd, in that I hadn't been sent anything of the sort in quite a while; what was nearly incomprehensible was my discovery, in the flyer's reflection in the glass living room table, of the now familiar calligraphy on its back, with its seemingly clumsy, thick block letters leaning toward the lower right corner of the paper.

Unlike the letter, the message was handwritten, not photocopied. It seemed to consist of two quotations:

"I cannot stand good old boys. If it depended on them, literature would have already disappeared from the face of the earth."

"I hate the vast majority of 'normal' human beings who day by day are destroying my world. I hate people who are very good-natured because no one has given them the opportunity to know what evil is and so to choose good freely; I have always thought that such good-natured people have an extraordinary malice in the making."

To say that the arrival of these messages astonished me would at this point be an understatement. The truth is that whoever was writing to me had a special gift for getting under my skin. Both quotes would have interested me under any circumstances, in a book, in the press, or at a conference. I thought I could see clues in them both to the history of whoever was writing to me and to my own life. The note writer selected his (her?) texts (original or appropriated? I wasn't sure), glimpsing that they would be the objects of a common passion (and perhaps a shared survival strategy, too?). Maybe it was too much for me to say that I found myself in them, but they undoubtedly hit close enough to the mark for the series to begin turning into a sort of fabulous chain whose magic lay precisely in its transcendence of the ordinary notion of writing and reading a text. I was committed to this "story," which I couldn't stop reading until I came across its last word, or, what was more disconcerting and in this case thrilling, until I discovered its author.

Who was my pursuer? How could he (or she) know where I live and be familiar with my habits, my identity, my consciousness, and even the things that lurked in my dreams? As daunting as these questions were, the richness of the messages and my desire for fresh submissions overcame my sense of alarm.

I see a man taking out a trumpet in the lobby of the Hospital del Maestro. I'm on the sidewalk across the avenue and am watching him through the plate glass window. Next to him is an old man. The cool light makes his instrument look extraordinarily golden. His instrument case is very battered, its corners broken and faded. What's going on here? A trumpet in a hospital at night in San Juan? What story lies behind this vision?

D'Style. Brides and Grooms. The signs of businesses with their fabulous and so often pathetic messages. This lengthy urban text constitutes a sort of substitute for dialogue or description, a cartography of the words of so many anonymous people, set in plastic rectangles or turned into neon structures. Through them, desire speaks, but also tedium and lies. They are sentences in the novel of the city.

Yesterday, I went with Julia and her little boy Javier to the movies. (Julia, that unfinished story, set aside due to apathy and boredom. We separated three years ago, but from time to time, we still see each other and occasionally hop in the sack out of sheer loneliness and sheer self-delusion.) We went to one of the Río Hondo theaters to watch a children's film. I knew what I was getting myself into from the moment I agreed to go and had nothing but the lowest expectations for what lay ahead that afternoon.

Just as the shorts ended, a couple with two children sat down right behind us, even though the whole auditorium was empty. I suppose there are a lot of people who model their behavior in movie theaters on the hours they spend every day in front of the TV, so they think it's OK to talk out loud, to stand up, and to let their kids touch other people's collars, kick the backs of their chairs, and run through the aisles. I almost asked Julia to move, but then thought it didn't matter, in the long run there's no escaping such people.

On the screen, a kangaroo was running away with a jacket and a wad of cash belonging to a cartoon gangster (this was the exquisite confection that we had paid money to subject ourselves to). The appalling plot struck me as both unreal and predictable, but for our back-row neighbors, the film had become a thriller. It would take some patience to explain to them that they weren't watching a documentary; that the kangaroo hadn't been trained, as they thought; and that everything they were watching had been created on a computer, so there was no need to wonder how the kangaroo could jump so high.

It was ridiculous, a half-baked idea, but I became convinced that their stupidity was negatively affecting my life. It was aggressive, in a way. I know such people exist in every society, but in this society, practically everything seems to cater to them, to keep them from realizing how childish, inept, and miserable they are. The purpose of our government is to let them go through all the stages of their lives without facing their shortcomings. Shopkeepers design sales with them in mind. That's why hardly anyone makes demands, why a handful of ideas are lauded everywhere: family, the illusion of democracy, consumer appeal. I am excluded because these people exist.

I couldn't help noticing the names of the boys who never stopped tormenting Javier. The elder was called Ostec or Usbec—anyway, something extraterrestrial-sounding, like parsec. The other had been christened with a name that most likely was taken straight from a soap opera. He was Jonathan Louis.

I knew I really did care about them, when I got down to it. All I had to do was imagine what it meant to be born and to grow up in a suburb in Bayamón, have names like those, spend whole years going from the Canton Mall to the Plaza Río Hondo, belong to the political party that allows for the highest level of self-hatred disguised as progress and hope, peddle products that promise bulging muscles or gleaming auto finishes, and every Sunday attend the church that has all the answers and the greatest music. I was definitely as much a person of this place as they were. They were, despite appearances, my compatriots.

I left the theater with the sensation I've had so often: the pain that never goes away, that I hardly even feel any more. But it's *always* there. Julia and I tried to put it into words but we soon gave up. The family in the theater, the drive along Highway 2 a few minutes later—there was no break between them. It was all the same. This was another part of the desert. Nothing set them apart. It was just more sand.

"Lookit, gimme two them big boxes." "I'm a tell you, here's her papers." "Don't you go changing." "Our prayers are getting through because the war isn't so bad." "You're gumming things up." "The wallet's the problem." "Wait up, I'm turning." "Dale una *pizza* con *mushrooms*." "It isn't cheap. It's expensive. I brought him a bunch of *biscotti*."

These are the things I hear and write down on the streets. Behind the words, the enigma remains. But everything smacks of plastic, of sun, of double-A batteries for a machine made in China. The only way out is having enough money to go into seclusion or to travel, recover by seeing and hearing other things. That's the only real privilege here. If you're rich enough, you can pretend you don't have anything to do with this.

I kept circling the block because I didn't want to stop listening to a program on Radio Universidad about a Cuban novelist, a schizophrenic, who went into exile in Miami and ended up committing suicide in the last decade of the twentieth century. His name (Wilson, William, I'm not sure) meant nothing to me. The critic they were interviewing recalled that he had destroyed almost everything he had written. A paragraph they read from a novel stuck with me. It told the story of the protagonist's arrival at the Miami airport from Cuba and the reaction of his family when they saw him. It said that they were expecting a man in the prime of life, a businessman, a future husband, father, and upstanding member of the exile community, yet what they met with was a prematurely aged man, toothless, looking at everyone with apprehension, who had to be committed on the very day he arrived to a psychiatric hospital.

When the reading ended, I felt overwhelmed. It was one of

those texts that nails the Caribbean. It proved the power of the fragmentary, how much can be said without the fanfare. That afternoon, I was spontaneously discovering a text of the same caliber as the ones I was being sent. This was good enough for me to send to myself; if I were daring enough, I might even send it to my pursuer.

I've often seen him in the small shopping center where the coffee shop is. Some of the richest housing developments in the metropolitan area are near there. He must still be living in one of those tracts, still with his parents, probably in his childhood bedroom. Despite his studies, or at least his attempts along those lines, he never managed to get a job or live independently. So he's come to be a bald, pot-bellied forty-year-old. Today, he's by himself, sharply dressed. Other times, he's in shorts and sandals, displaying a slovenliness you don't often see in his circles. He comes around here at the most ungodly hours, so he clearly has no job, no work to do; he's a moocher, dead broke. I've seen how the coffee shop workers make fun of him, probably thinking there's something deeply unfair about this waste of privilege. The man pretends not to notice their contempt, so thick you could cut it, and keeps on walking.

I just saw someone parking a car the same color and model as mine. For a second, I thought I was watching myself arrive. The thought came so naturally, as if it were actually possible, as if there weren't anything demented about that perception.

I'm looking at the floodlights in the park where I played baseball as a boy. Back then I got to see them being built. This was more than thirty years ago. They're the same towers I struck with the best hit of my career. The ball bounced off into a bit of swampy pasture, all that was left of what the whole area must have been until it was developed in the 1940s or 50s.

The same towers, the same trees, the same bit of primordial

habitat, the same consciousness. Eternity must be pretty much like this.

When I recall visits to the Santa Rosa shopping center in Bayamón, it's always the middle of summer and the sun is beating down on a merciless cement pavement, an image of desolation. Inside, the short passageway with shops on either side is dark, dank, immune to air conditioning.

When my father was dying, I went to buy myself a pair of shoes like the ones he wore. I'd just broken them in when he passed away. The leather soles were very slippery. That was how I walked for weeks following his death, wearing shoes that could have been his, constantly on the verge of toppling.

The boy was sitting on a cement bench opposite the entrance to an office building. He must have come from school, as his schoolbook backpack was in front of him, and he must have been waiting for someone to come pick him up. Maybe eleven or twelve years old, a little small for his age, unkempt hair, wearing a silver bracelet on his right wrist, too big for him, too incongruent on a small boy. I was having a cup of coffee a few steps away, at the counter in a tiny coffee shop. He was staring fixedly at some point, both at the ground right in front of him and at something far away. I felt certain that I must have been like him, that this combination of fragility and cool was the face I once offered the world. I knew, then, what he would go through later, what his lost stare already suspected: the inability to understand the desires and the violence of everyone else; the riddle of finding so many people so sure of themselves, ready to accept the world, who later dissolve into drab adults with various degrees of remorse and ignorance. I knew that this was what awaited him. His stare seemed to have a presentiment of it that afternoon. I had an impulse to keep this boy from suffering, but all I did was finish my coffee and leave.

Something occurred to me that, at least for the moment, has invigorated me: I should be sending my own messages. Whoever keeps pestering me is familiar with my routines and particulars. All I have to do is leave him or her an envelope or a note taped to my office or any other place where they know I go. I thought I might write down what I remembered about the Cuban novelist. I have nothing to lose by complicating the game, by making it mine as well. I should write the text. When I've got it, I'll see if I do it.

Today, I found this written in colored chalk on the asphalt in front of my car in the university parking lot: "Today I am defeated, as if I had learned the truth." My pursuer must be dedicated and have some free time and guts because it must have gone through his mind that I might discover him. I went to the guard's booth and asked if he had seen anyone writing something on the ground. I had to repeat the question and explain it until it gave me a sensation of being ridiculous. And no one enjoys being taken for an imbecile or a crazy person.

Going back to my car, I found a piece of yellow paper caught under the windshield wiper. Just a couple of minute earlier, when I read the message on the ground, there hadn't been anything on the windshield. I pretended to be uninterested in the folded note and didn't look up because I didn't want to encounter the eyes of my message writer. I wasn't ready just then. I was stuck between fury and fright.

I left the parking lot as quickly as I could. I didn't know whether my seeming lack of interest would deceive my pursuer. It was to be expected that he had been spying on me, and knowing that he was so nearby was intolerable for me. I thought some signal from me was expected and that I'd squandered my chance to send it. The messages, their delivery, and the skill with which it was all done were starting to feel like a seduction, and I didn't know what to do with that.

I took a roundabout way home. Stupidly, with a mixture of pleasure and terror, I imagined that I was being followed. For what? Why? It was impossible to know.

When I came in and closed the door, I realized I hadn't opened the sheet of yellow paper. There was the usual calligraphy, the coarsely yet carefully drawn print letters, angling down toward the right margin. "Walter Benjamin said that in our time the only work truly endowed with meaning—critical meaning, as well—would have to be a collage of quotations, excerpts, echoes of other works."

I wandered between the kitchen and the other rooms, in the dark, not making any noise, trying my best to give no sign that might give away my presence. Several times, I went to the corner of the window, where I could hide behind the curtains and peer out. The street was the same as ever, the same neighbors I barely exchanged greetings with, the usual barking dogs, the symmetrically arranged cones of streetlight.

Today, on a street in Río Piedras, a man in a T-shirt walked by me. When he was near, I saw the date printed on the cloth: September 23, 1977. The T-shirt was announcing an event that took place a quarter of a century ago. I recalled an anecdote I once heard Diego tell. He knew a member of the Socialist Party who, after an event where few people had shown up, took a box of T-shirts that they wouldn't be selling again home with him. He used them for years with complete indifference, with demented frugality.

I had just met that man, who was no longer young, who had probably been walking around the city's streets for years bearing on his chest the vestiges of a vanished world.

I was invited to take part in a conference titled "The Right to Raise a Stink." I've always been surprised by the simulated populism of the way organizers name so many intellectual activities, as if they were making a commitment or, worse, they felt embarrassed that the great majority of people find this sort of work unnecessary and incomprehensible. I suppose they're trying to show that, despite appearances, the participants are just like anybody else. Nevertheless, the people who go to these events are hardly average folks, and I've never run into anyone from my own street at one of them.

I find it hard to attend these events. I'd rather read a text than have to listen to it, and besides, I rarely come across a talk that I find truly illuminating. This time I got there for the opening keynote and stayed for hours, waiting for my turn, witnessing a series of funeral dirges.

There was a bit of everything, from the reading of some fairly worthwhile texts to the recitations of others that became unbearable because of their authors' efforts to cite without restraint a half dozen international luminaries, whose appearance in these writings was disturbingly predictable. I imagined how astonished those major figures would be if they found fragments of their works used by scholars from all five continents to support the most unlikely topics and conclusions.

Sometimes this repeated appeal to authority was suspicious, sometimes merely a nervous tic. One anthropologist with an authentic Cuban accent and questionable hair color demonstrated an oddly open interpretation of Lacan's seminar on psychoses in the longwinded and disquieting conclusion to her commentary on the hundredth anniversary of the Universidad de Puerto Rico. Then there was the frightening sociologist Carmen Lindo, who, instead of pronouncing Derrida in the French way, with the accent on the last syllable, alluded to the philosopher three or four dozen times over the space of fifteen dense and impenetrable pages with the accent on the first syllable and a trilled *r*: "Dérida." To top it off, she cited "Dérida" in an English translation, which for the public's benefit she followed with a spontaneous version in Spanish that suffered a bit too much from trial and error.

There was also a lawyer-historian who, after saying he didn't want to presume to predict the future, ran half an hour out of time and out of sense in giving us a detailed description of the coming century, which he was certain would be an age of solidarity. Also noteworthy was the second talk by professor Lindo, who, each time (and there were many times) she quoted her sources and found that they had written "man" to refer to humanity, would offer her generous aid by chiming in with "and I would add woman," thus creating spontaneous, unauthorized collaborative texts, which, while contributing little, at least showed her taking some risks and presenting her own words, predictable and obsessive as they may have been.

That's how I spent my day, dreaming of coffee breaks, incredulous to find someone capable of citing Deleuze and Gabriela Mistral in the same sentence just like that, without forewarning or footnotes, yoked together by a conjunction that both linked and disfigured their meaning. I skipped the farewells and left before the end, having heard the prodigious citer of "Dérida" preface her commentary on the final panel by warning us that she had "only nine little points to make." In the end, a day of ordeals that will have to be filed under the heading "Conferences Attended," in the hopes that it will prove of some use in the fateful hour when contracts are renewed at the university.

Diego is off on another trip. He dropped by to give me the keys to his house. He has a crew of workers remodeling the kitchen and bedrooms, and he wants me to stay on top of them. He spends less and less time in San Juan, lately no more than three or four days at a stretch, and it's very likely that the bank he works for will send him for an extended time to some large South American city. I don't know why he's investing money in a house he won't be living in. I miss my friend, who I feel is growing more and more distant, who I see disassociating himself from the world that was ours for so many years.

It's Saturday and night has fallen. I've gone to his house to check on the how the work is going. I doubt the workers have done anything this afternoon; there's no sign they've been here. Everything's covered in a layer of cement dust and the electricity is shut off to part of the house. I'm sitting on the kitchen floor, near the lamp that used to be in the living room and that has now been tossed in some corner here, next to a cushion leaning incongruently against the fridge.

It isn't my house, but I've been coming here for years. The construction work has made it less familiar, but the place is still part of my past. Nevertheless, in the silence tonight, in this abandoned, dusty house, I feel anxious. There's something disturbing and secretive about being here. Coming to this residence, which the construction has transformed into ruins, writing under this single light bulb, listening to the noise of the wind, the distant murmurs of the neighbors, I get nervous and jumpy, and I know this feeling has nothing to do with my doing Diego a favor. I've come here so I won't have to be home or in a shop where everyone can see me. Nobody could imagine me here. I'm hidden. Here no messages will arrive.

I've gone into the bathroom and found Virginia Woolf's diary in a pile of books. It can't belong to Diego. It must be some of the stuff one of his women left behind. I've opened it at random and read the first line of a paragraph. I've copied it in the notebook, imitating as best I could the block letters that have been pursuing me for weeks.

"I must note the symptoms of the disease, so as to know it next time."

In a while I'll leave. I'll tear the sheet from the notebook, fold it in half, and when I get home I'll stick it in the brown envelope I got a few days ago and place it under the windshield wiper, where I always park my car.

In my notebook, the sentence no longer means what it did in Woolf's diary, and it will signify something even more different when it's in the envelope waiting for the mystery hand.

A few words extracted from a diary, now turned into the beginnings of a dialogue. The irony is not lost on me.

Now gripping a walker, the elderly man takes his place in line at a diner in old San Juan. Twenty years ago he spent his nights at the Burger King on Calle San Francisco, next to a guy from the United States with a shaved head who would sit at the same table and read the Bible. How many years in this city have I watched how these people's stories serve to knit my own together?

I've placed the Woolf quotation in the last envelope they sent me and stuck it on the windshield. I can't help feeling distressed and a bit ridiculous. The bait is set. I'm aware that, with this act, I'm taking on a new position in the game; that by doing this, I'm recognizing what's been happening; and that doing this may mean that everything will change.

Writing fragments, writing notes in a notebook as the days fly by, is the closest I can come to creating a text that doesn't know it's lying. Later, when I rework it, I'll introduce subterfuges and establish ways of not saying things, or of not saying everything. But here, in this black notebook, I still don't know what I shouldn't let myself confess. It doesn't matter if what I say is true. I don't need to know. I don't know what will happen tomorrow. I don't know what I'll write after that. I've got all my writing ahead of me.

My message elicited no response. I've been dreaming. I thought they'd see it right away. Perhaps it is the case that they're following me, but nobody can shadow me twenty-four hours a day. I finally took the envelope from the windshield, and in an ultimate act of inanity, I fixed it to the lid of the mail box. There the afternoon showers destroyed it.

I went to meet a colleague at the Universidad del Sagrado Corazón. While I was walking along a corridor past the classrooms, I saw a large sign taped to a blackboard: "Be brief. I want to share." Given its location, it was a call to a supposedly democratic superficiality and the militant slogan of those who are incapable of listening and understanding but who demand participation. Nevertheless, because of what I had been going through, the sign seemed aimed at me. All around me, I found messages, even if I wasn't supposed to be the addressee. Wasn't this absurd suggestion from a university classroom what I wanted to communicate to my pursuer? Hadn't I been trying to hobble them, to put a limit on them, to shut them up, to replace their voice (which was beginning to appear excessive to me) with my own? Wasn't that what I'd been trying to do when I put an envelope on my car's windshield?

—Talk to me, pops!

—A coffee and toast, I say.

—Two coffees, but make 'em real *Yaucono*, ordered the man standing next to me, using the brand name as if it were a commercial. His name was Frank, and he was flirting with the waitress: a frankly horrific, middle-aged woman.

I see a couple leaving the coffee shop.

—I got something to do, the guy said distractedly. He was about twenty and obviously dying to get out of there.

—*¡Dame un* fucking *beso!* says the girl, grabbing him in a forced embrace.

Later, in another coffee shop, I discover that the waitress, a fake-blond Puerto Rican, is named Amadora. I have to wait to give her my order because she and a client are trying to resolve the mystery of why his *cortadito* tastes bad.

—It's 'cause I whipped the milk, says Amadora, clarifying nothing. Even so, I risk another café con leche.

A few minutes later the older man, probably a retiree, who had been talking with Amadora and who I can now see through the window, opens his car door and vomits. Just two spurts, a thin puke that lies on the sidewalk like a puddle of water.

The next day, in the afternoon, at Cafetería Mallorca in old San Juan, I order a cup of café con leche, which they make in their antique coffee machine. I watch the waitress while she makes it. She pours the milk from a dented metal jug with the brand written on a small black label: "Colony Economy."

My life has passed me by in this "Colony Economy," rehearsing the coffee ritual as if it were some kind of barrier against a torrent of history that overwhelms and defines me. What is left of the men and women of this country? What remains but the coffee and the centuries, ground down and percolated, flowing through steel tubes, pouring from plastic spigots?

In a bookstore, I find an anthology of pieces about the problems that come from feeling too small. I've met its author—a scrounger, a survivor of multiple financial catastrophes—and I'm aware of the extremes to which he'd go. The text is such a travesty that I'm tempted to buy it. Instead, I go for copying a few lines from *San Sebastián de las Vegas del Pepino: The Basis of Pepinian Ethnicity: Brief Reflective Essays*. (Are there essays of the unreflective variety?) The note on the back cover tells us a little about the book and its author: "Juan Valcárcel del Pino is a Pepinian writer who proposes a new terminology of his own, drawing on research from the field of ideas, sociology, and the popular apperception of culture to prove that Pepinianity exists as a psycho-spiritual phenomenon that takes concrete form as a philosophical principal. This book gives Pepinianity a physical, social, and, at the same time, a transcendent status. It invites all Pepinians to transcend in their appreciation and support for the physical, social, cultural, and spiritual heritage of San Sebastián del Pepino."

Farther on, the reader is informed that the book is "an analysis of how Pepinians should gain transcendent perception in light of the processes and values that gave rise to and sustain the Pepino Collective."

Also deserving honorable mention are the titles of a couple of chapters: "I. Original Status of the Pepino Future" and "X. Pepinianism: Pepinophilia and the Pepinophile."

I guess the government of this small town in the western part of the country must have paid to have it published. I also guess it is understood that this is how cultural works get done here. It is also clear that the book was written to be read by no one, merely to exist.

So many years on the same streets. It occurs to me that it is here where I have thought through the great questions of life, on afternoons that always seem like summer, intolerably hot and boring, at the intersection of Avenida Ponce de León and Domenech, in front of the Asociación de Empleados del ELA, or crossing Andalucía street where the low, claustrophobic buildings of Caparra Terrace offer no shade. Such questions always arise in unlikely places. Nevertheless, there are things I should never have inquired about under this sun or while crossing this cement desert. These questions have made me feel San Juan as I feel no other city on earth, as I perhaps had to, to gain knowledge and a sense of disgust.

I run into a group of young people coming from the beach.

—You had a stiffy, says the girl, aged twelve or thirteen.

—Me? Answers the boy.

—Not now! A while ago. You had a stiffy.

—Me?

The repetition of the answer is weak and shows that the girl was right.

—I don't care. I call it like I see it. I'm saying you had a stiffy.

—Hello.

I looked up from the notebook where I had been writing. It was an Asian girl who held out her hand and told me her name too fast for me to catch.

—Glad to meet you, I said, putting down my pen and hastening to shake her hand.

—I like what you do.

—Thanks. Would you like to sit.

—I can't. Good-bye.

She offered me her hand again. Her black, straight hair fell across her face, obscuring it. I watched her back as she walked away from the Starbucks next to the bookstore in San Patricio Plaza. Not bad looking.

A new message has arrived in the most banal way possible, by mail. I have to confess I had been waiting impatiently, expecting one to come by less conventional methods. There are two parts to it. First there is the name of an author I don't know, followed, as in a bibliography, by texts he has written. The titles are ridiculous, yet sadly plausible. It is all written on a typewriter or in a computer font that imitates typewriting, and most likely, it's a fragment torn from a document and then photocopied. Then, at the bottom, in the usual block letters, comes a phrase that also seems to be a quotation.

"Vicente Molina Ruiz, 'Seven Columns on Education'
, 'Foundations of Freedom'
, 'The ABCs of Critical Thinking'
, 'Great Puerto Ricans for History'
He knew that only permutation secures us the truth."

The light, the morning impressions that San Juan leaves when you've had to be in an office building long enough to become familiar with the dynamics of people entering and leaving, the route of the coffee cart, or the temperature changes sparked by the air conditioning. The sensation (very subjective, but perhaps shared) of feeling so close, physically and conceptually, to a stand crammed with magazines in Spanish that thousands, perhaps hundreds of thousands, of people will read in the Caribbean, Central America, and the rest of Latin America. Monthlies that I don't buy or read, but that make me feel that I belong to this world. The sensation starts with the yellow light, with the sunbeams creating columns of dust pointed skyward and slicing through the morning, in the middle of a traffic jam, amid noxious gas and honking horns on this morning, which has been the same as far back as I can remember.

How many years crossing Río Piedras, from the Plaza del Mercado to the bookstores? Today I pay attention to Calle Monseñor Torres, which starts at the entrance to the Plaza, just beyond the lottery men and street sellers setting out their wares every morning, in the human-scale anthill (its rawness, its extraordinary freight of reality) that is Río Piedras. On the short Calle Monseñor Torres, beggars hail one another from corner to corner and a record store blasts the street with a song by La India. It would seem, despite the chaos, that everything was in its place: the crowd of men missing legs in their wheelchairs, the "Miss Millennium Model" ads, the neopsychedelic decoration in Cafetería Los Amigos, the row of timbales in the shop window of Casa Isern, the clock on the Tren Urbano station, the apartment buildings looking out on the Plaza de la Convalecencia where, if Río Piedras had been different, I would have liked to live.

I head in the direction of El Amal pharmacy. I smell cigar smoke, the kind with a hint of vanilla that they sell at a kiosk in the Plaza del Mercado. It takes me a few seconds to realize that the smoker is the old man walking ahead of me. He's shouting something I can't understand. He carries two shopping bags, calling out to the people on foot and in their cars. He tirelessly repeats the word or phrase that I can't make out. *"¡Cheneychequer!"* Incongruently, I think of the vice-president of the United States, but a second later I notice that the bags he's carrying hold boxes of *damas chinas*—that is, Chinese checkers. I leave him behind and another older man comes to mind who a few minutes ago had been drinking his coffee next to me in the coffee shop in the plaza. He poured an enormous amount of sugar into his cup. The stream of sugar flowed for seconds. It was astonishing how much he could drink, in three or four gulps. So many things have always seemed unbelievable to me, as if the world were endlessly foreign to me, as if this were the measure of the distance between me and the men I share it with.

What are these streets but my own life? Time circulating like water or wind, a body that will keep growing smaller and more fragile, alongside the gutters that flow always in the same direction, along the road that also is mine. Cities matter more to those who go in the same direction as their gutters, those who travel at their level. No master of this city—none of its mayors—care about this city as I've cared about it because I know that I have no way out, that I'll never be able to leave. Not even exile would free me of San Juan. I'd simply suffer doubly: for belonging to the city and for being far from it.

The new message was almost erased by the afternoon showers. The black ink of the block letters was running like mascara smeared by tears. The mystery man or woman is running out of strategies for getting them to me because they are starting to repeat. The message, however, has some new elements: it is in English, it is a question (possibly addressed to me), and it contains the name of a French street.

"Remember me at rue Falguière?"

That street, Falguière, wasn't far from where I lived in Paris. However, I rarely went there, since my usual destinations lay in other directions. But why the question? And most of all, who could know that I had lived in that neighborhood?

I could barely call up an image of that road. My memories of Paris were so faded that I was surprised to recall it had once been the center of my world. Maybe that was precisely why, having once thought it indispensable, I now found it one of the farthest removed corners of the planet.

It was hard, therefore, to recall a person, when I could barely recall the place of our hypothetical encounter. Whoever was writing to me was doing it by chapters. I was sure that more clues were on the way.

I'm sitting on the floor writing in this notebook, next to a crib where a month-old baby sleeps. I've come looking for some documents in the house that once belonged to my aunt and uncle, where my cousin lives now with her husband and children. She's asked me to watch her sleeping newborn so she can run out to buy milk and diapers. In this room, which her son has only just begun to recognize, I spent many of my childhood days. No doubt that is why I've sat down here, specifically in this corner of the room, where I used to play hide-and-seek with the cousin I'm now waiting for, though I have no intention of ever seeing her again, at least not so long as her husband continues to be the great distributor of wheeled utility shelving units.

I never imagined I'd have the opportunity to be back on the same terrazzo tiles that my feet trod as a boy, in this corner, my back leaning against the wall that I threw balls at for hours, fighting off weariness, dreaming of the glories of baseball and basketball players. My unexpected return to this place helps me measure the weight of my burdens. Once, I was that boy, and once, my cousin was one of the people I loved most in the world.

The mobile-shelf magnate hands me the newspaper, probably figuring he should fill the five minutes of conversation time he's set aside for me by mocking some protesters:

"A group of sympathizers encouraged them not to come down from the tree, at least two exchanges of words arising with the superintendent of police. A third protester opted to climb to the highest point of the tree, and two rescue squad members were sent up in the basket to make him come down. The ambulances, which had been late in arriving, were in place, and nearby, the mayor of San Juan even made an appearance, and farther away, three statehood sympathizers shouted terrorists and potheads at the protesters."

I meet the smile of my cousin's husband when I lift my eyes from the page. Apart from the inept prose, what we have here is the usual vacuity. The undeveloped drama that won't get past the first act and will end in the customary outcome: the ancient tree felled by unknown hands in the predawn hours some Mother's Day or Good Friday; a superintendent and a mayor representing the interests of those who have always won, steamrolling sensitivity, intelligence, and courage, convinced simultaneously that they embody morality and that this will get them the funds for retiring in a US city where they might even feel solidarity with the people who protect the trees. But not here, here it isn't worth it, here we deserve this atrocity.

In a filthy bathroom, I see graffiti, scrawled in English, that says, "The Panty Sniffers." It boasts the usual inanity of these toilet writings, supplemented on this occasion by the falsity of its expression of desire, for in the next line it adds in Spanish, "Not because I want to, I do it to please you."

I returned home while night was falling this rainy Friday night. As I walked in, my eye was immediately drawn to the blinking red light on the answering machine. Few people have my number, and still fewer call it. My pursuer took the trouble to record a female computer-generated voice (those generic, spectral voices with extravagant vibrations at the end of the syllables) with the following message: "FROM WHICH REMARKABLY ENOUGH NOTHING DEVELOPS." I've written it in all caps because that's how it sounded. At this point in the game, I hardly needed to worry about how my pursuer got my number.

I grow befuddled every day in trying to discover a hint that might reveal the identity of the message writer, and I suspect it must be someone I know. But I hope it isn't, hope that his hiding behind words and stratagems might finally be the good news that this society with no surprises is giving me.

Nevertheless, lurking in this message is life's abomination: *nothing will come of this*. The matter will remain incomplete, like a frustrated hope. Perhaps one day, as mysteriously as they appeared, the messages will disappear. I should expect nothing. That is what good sense and experience tell me, but I cannot bow down before my conclusions.

This Sunday, I saw Máximo Noreña looking like the devil, on his way out of a crowded shopping center. He stood with two children who must be his sons, waiting, holding a bag from K-Mart, while they finished eating a pretzel. He seemed totally fed up. He is an author who matters to me, but none of the hundreds who surrounded him had the slightest idea of his work. I crossed the street slowly, feeling the asphalt yield under my footsteps, softened by the sun on this hateful summer afternoon. Looking at him, I could see myself a few years from now. He knows nothing of my admiration. We've never been introduced. Seeing him there, so miserable, I felt my appreciation and fascination grow. Seeing the banal and terrible despair of an afternoon like this, you can begin to understand the demons of this city and this country. He has not stopped writing about them, as if he had nothing else to hold onto if he wants to survive.

Under my office door, I found a little flyer for a rock band called Los Pepiniyoz. Their symbol is a big question mark drawn in a thick stroke circled by a delicate line. The flyer contained the usual information: date, time, address of the concert venue. It sat on my desk all afternoon without my realizing there was a message on the back. It must be a quote; I'd like to assume that it's a quote because it would be scary if my pursuer could read my mind so well.

"You write because you like to, because you do not know how to do anything else, because you are unable to get your revenge by any other means. But in no way does this weakness for the text make you blind to the superfluity of your labors."

There is a diner in Río Piedras that already has the tables set at eleven in the morning, with red plastic tablecloths and paper napkins held down by the weight of the silverware. Entering, I find an extraordinarily large surface surrounded by chairs. I realize it is the pool table and that people also sit here to eat.

Years ago I spent one summer afternoon gathering the mangos I found lying on the pavement in Luis Muñoz Marín Park. In the end, I filled two shopping bags that I found discarded there. I was with my girlfriend, a woman I had lived with for some time before our relationship fell apart. This was the last time we went out together. I remember the futility of that afternoon: running all over the park picking up overripe fruit. We filled our bags with mangos much as we might have filled them with paper smeared with bits of food or with empty cans. It was better than having to talk. It was our mute good-bye.

A few days later, I would set out her last belongings (the ones my girlfriend didn't want to take with her) for the garbage truck, along with the bags full of mangos, which had rotted. We hadn't even bothered to taste them.

I've been told that a group of friends (lawyers, accountants, shopkeepers with literary inclinations) get together in a coffee shop every Sunday to discuss the newspapers. I am told that they roar with laughter.

I've totaled up all the places I've lived in. No doubt I missed a few, but there's only so much you can ask from me. Nevertheless, I remember perfectly well the ritual I went through every time I time moved out. With each apartment, I assumed I'd be staying in place for a long time, but I never did. When I was all packed up to move, just before I shut the door and turned in the key, I'd go inside for a moment and say good-bye to the walls. Sometimes I thanked them; frequently I cursed them. In any case, it was always a farewell, as if the apartments had been witnesses.

Julia invited me to her house. After lunch, she had to go out, and she asked me to babysit Javier for a while. We watched cartoons and then played hide-and-seek. I'm hiding behind the sofa when I come face-to-face with the child, who's holding a photo of his mother in front of himself as if it were an icon. I ask him to show it to me. I don't recognize it; it's a photo from before we met. Julia is smiling into the camera, and her hair is very long. Javier takes me by the hand to the bedroom. He's gone under the bed and taken out a shoebox full of photographs. I sit down to look at them with him. I recognize some of them because Julia had shown them to me when we were together, but apparently, there are many others she didn't want me to see. She appears with people I've never met, sitting in apartments I knew nothing about, wearing haircuts and makeup that reveal a side of her I never glimpsed. In some of them she radiates an irrefutable beauty and looks straight at the camera, convinced of her power.

There are dozens: groups circled around family tables, moments immortalized on the streets of old San Juan with a bottle of beer in her hand, or on the beach in a baseball cap, a seed necklace and a yellow bikini. At the bottom of the box, probably placed there on purpose, is a group in which she appears naked in unmade beds and of close-ups of her face looking at the camera through tender, half-closed eyes. I understand that these are the photos she let other men take of her. I discover, while Javier plays with a robot next to me, that these images never could have been mine, or ours.

"Simone Weil taught philosophy to the railway workers at a night school on rue Falguière." So said the computerized female voice on my answering machine. Simone Weil? The French philosopher? I remembered nothing about her except that she had been a sort of saint for the left. Is this message a clue about the sex of its sender? For days, I've had the feeling that something is changing. I know I might be mistaken, but the vibes I get from this message seem to confirm this transformation. Simone, like the Simone of one of the first messages? Simone Weil? Is this a signature? Who are you? Why are you looking for me?

I find this article tacked up in a bus station on Avenida Ponce de León. It shows the self-demeaning insanity that seems to be part and parcel of this society:

"The separatists, from the most leftist derivatives of communists (there are no communists anymore but their ideas and theories are still around, especially the materialist method of analysis), the nationalists, the anti-American and the pro-American separatists have many differences, but they have one thing in common, they base their separatism on the idea that the Nation is the land, the utopian or ideological idea, and not its people.

"Is it being a Patriot to plant bombs and kill innocent compatriots or the negative and destructive criticism that kills the spirits of people who work, the effect being nearly identical? Is it being a Patriot in the new modality of ecoterrorists with their extremist demands of 'environmentalism' without trying to find a balance of benefits or harm to the citizenry and the environment?

"Thinking that Patriotism is just a walk in the park, or criticizing in a negative and destructive way, which are bombs that kill the positivism and creativity of the citizenry, is not being a Patriot, it is being a Patrioteer."

How could I not fantasize that the person sending me messages is a woman—a woman I could fall in love with—when I'm surrounded by people capable of producing texts such as this? How could I not find hope in this seduction by words? How not dream of an unknown body that is utterly unlike these voices assailing me, voices that have nothing to do with me and nothing to tell me, which will never understand me, until having to share my life with them feels like a form of dying, of having been dying day by day throughout my entire life?

I didn't notice until today that the article I picked up at the bus station includes a request at the bottom: "Print it Forward it to 20 to photocopy and they forward it to 20 more and they talk about it with 20 more." How can I be sure that the person sending me the messages is writing exclusively to me? Couldn't he or she be sending them, like the fanatic who goes around posting his allegations all over the city, to lots of people? Might I not be part of a network of victims, of a spectacle, of a work of art, or of a dirty joke?

I borrowed a CD of Arvo Pärt from Diego and played it in the car on the way to work. After just a few minutes, I came close to turning it off and tuning into the news. The music frightened me. I didn't know the name of the piece; the CD was a burned copy that only gave the composer's name. It must have been a requiem because the powerful chorus brought up waves of emotion that had been buried since who knows when.

Listening to it, I pictured my death on Avenida Central between San Patricio and Río Piedras—from the discovery of a cancer (in the pancreas or liver, one of the terrible, silent ones) to the last agony. I was listening to the music and experiencing my hopelessness, the malaise that would make existence intolerable and that would be expressed in my refusal to get treatment. That was the emotion that has been bottled up inside me for years, a swelling agitation that I didn't know where to direct, which shook me to my core. Thus, between Avenida de Diego and Calle Andalucía, I confronted the banality of my death. The purpose of the music's beauty was to produce this. Its art was to console those who await defeat.

I got to work still reeling from the impact of the music, and on entering my office I found a new message. The block letters were slanted rightward as usual and again precisely on target: "He knew that only permutation would secure him the truth." This time the message came on the back of a bibliography; the phrase was written out and numbered one hundred times, as if it were some old school punishment.

I burst into the department office and, under the astonished gazes of the secretaries, left as abruptly as I'd entered. I badgered the people in the neighboring offices and checked my floor of the building to see if I could find anyone suspicious. Nobody knew or had seen anything. I didn't want to go into details because I didn't want them asking me what was up. But with my emotions so stirred, I could no longer be passive; I needed clarity. Waiting wasn't good enough. "He knew that only permutation would secure him the truth." What did that signify? How could someone fire into the air and hit the bull's-eye? What truth was I afraid of? Why were the permutations undergone by the messages beginning to alarm me? Who could know me so well as to predict the movements of my mind? I was already old enough and cynical enough to take cabals and mysteries seriously. But how could I have a message waiting for me that expressed what I had experienced when I was sitting in a car driving from one end of Avenida Central to the other while listening to a CD that belonged to someone in Caracas? These messages had never been a joking matter, and for some time now, they'd started to worry me, admit it or not. Nevertheless, fear and fascination live at the same address. I scrutinized the faces of the people I crossed paths more closely than ever. Any one of them might be the person stalking me.

There was a singer-songwriter, as I now recall, who began by writing melodies that others made famous and then, years later, ventured to record his own album. It was a hit, leading him to face an audience for the first time. He wasn't a great performer, but he became one of the indisputably important figures of his time.

Ever since I heard his story, I've been struck by the steps he took, his halting, measured introduction of himself to other people. Now, I'm relating this to the person sending me these messages, though perhaps the story has more to do with me and my relationships with others. I've spent my life carefully measuring out my ties with my fellow man, as if full, direct, and immediate contact would be too much. How many things have taken me too long because of my hesitation and throat clearing? Then again, how long have I taken to get out of certain matters and relationships? My life has passed by while I've kept strangers at a prudent distance. I've seen them as invaders; that is why I've been a pair of watching eyes more than anything, the man who observes, keeping the possibility open of just walking on by. I've been like that singer-songwriter who introduced himself to his audience one step at a time.

I've sensed the pain in this room, grief gathered over years, generation upon generation, between these four walls. All afternoon here in this room, I've felt its eternity, convinced to a certainty that when I am gone my grief will live on, who knows how long, who knows for whom.

I've been thinking about certain streets and sidewalks: if the soles of my shoes were paint brushes, by this time my footsteps might have completely covered their surfaces. Absurd, as absurd as so many true ideas. And so, with my foot-brushes, these shoe-markers, I express the autobiographical city, the city whose body my own body has covered.

Yesterday, Julia called, and today, I've gone with her and Javier to a shopping center with stores that boast about their prices in Barceloneta. The drive took longer than it should have because, distracted, we didn't catch sight of it from the highway and got as far as Arecibo before doing a U-turn and backtracking.

I've experienced every extreme with Julia. Over a short lapse of time, we could go from a fulfilling life together to a sense that a sudden breakup was brewing. If she hadn't had a miscarriage, we would have a five or six year old son. I've heard this inanity from couples who would probably have become terrible parents, but it might have been good for us if that child had lived.

Answering Julia's calls, seeing her now and then, and not caring that she has a son by a man who shows up every once in a while—all this makes me wonder. I don't think fooling people into thinking we're a family over a whole afternoon helps any of us. Yet there we were, still going out together because yesterday was Saturday and we had nothing else to do.

We went into stores where Julia tried on whole racks of clothes, leaving me to watch Javier. We went to look at furniture as if we were thinking about redecorating a house that didn't exist. I bought Javier a new robot. We lingered in front of jewelry stores and at a travel agency window; we remarked how expensive tickets had gotten to cities that we'd never visit. Before heading back, we swung by the fast food court.

When I stopped at her house, I helped her with the stroller and the sleeping child, and in the end, I went up to the half of the upstairs apartment where she lives. We made love out of habit, almost indolently. Afterward, I fell asleep even though I knew Julia wouldn't want to have me there the next morning when Javier woke up.

In the early dawn half-light, we shared a pot of coffee. On the stairs, in parting, I gave her money to buy her child another toy. Much more than she would have needed.

It was odd to be up on a Sunday at that hour. San Juan was empty. The silence and solitude of the rising light created the impression of the aftermath of some unknown disaster. The sun was coming out in force, and the day would be hot, as always. I had all the hours of Sunday ahead of me and didn't know what to do with them. For a moment, I was tempted to make a U-turn, go back to Julia's house, say I was sorry for something, no idea what, and stay there. But the day promised to be too hot, and I wanted to sleep.

The next weekend we went out again. This time, we went to Naguabo to have dinner by the little dilapidated pier.

Julia was happy. We had talked over the phone during the week and were looking forward to Saturday with some anticipation. On the way to the coastal village, we had a conversation without falling into the old traps, and I drove for quite a while with her hand on mine.

As we were driving into the village, I committed the indiscretion of mentioning the messages.

—So there's a crazy woman out there stalking you, she said without weighing the effect of her words, as if an emergency alarm had started howling in her head, stifling any playfulness, irony, or trust.

—That's not what I'm saying. Besides, I don't even know whether it's a woman, I replied.

—That's not what you just said.

—I don't think it's that simple.

—It's obvious. I don't know what you're telling me this for.

The truth is that I didn't either. The easy answer was, well, I had to tell somebody. No sooner had I come up with this miserable explanation than I realized something inside me was rebelling against the possibility of starting a new relationship with Julia. The fact that everything might turn out fine on this day was no relief; it would only mean draining the bitter cup of disaster a second time.

At the restaurant, wrapped up in our mute turmoil, we pretended to be the family we weren't. I remembered the photos in the shoebox, her face captured by men she had given herself to and who had left. There are some people destined never to find peace, and I was sure Julia was one. Nothing, no one, could stop this process, which had begun who knows when. Our life together had been a constant grind, and there on the rooftop terrace of the restaurant, I clearly saw we'd never amount to anything but a tangle of impossible demands. We wouldn't change. I never again wanted to hear complaints about a grief that was not my own.

I watched how, almost turning her back to me, she slowly stripped the fish of its meat. She cut small pieces to put in her son's mouth while looking at the boats in the fishing harbor and out to the sea that spread from here to Venezuela with nothing in between. We both knew that this outing had been a mistake.

After lunch, obstinately refusing to admit how deeply we were frustrated, we went to the beach in Humacao. Javier played in the sand while, without looking at each other, we exchanged brief phrases that brought no relief.

Later, when night was falling, the highway became an enormous tunnel that I entered rather than having to contend with the people in the back seat. Sometimes Julia would say something, and I'd answer reluctantly, not caring whether she could hear me. The day had been shot for hours, and I was beyond communicating with Julia or anybody else. This was a sensation I'd known before, one that always hit me with alarming exuberance. I knew that nothing but sleep, whenever it finally came, would calm me.

Getting out of the car in front of her two-story building, Julia took the boy and the stroller out and went upstairs without saying good-bye.

I drove around the city in the drizzling rain. The houses, the low-paying jobs, the women came back to me. On these ribbons of pavement, I had experienced dreams and disappointments, but at my age now, it was all too much.

I stopped at a gas station to buy a beer. Next to the cash register they had cigars. I almost bought one but didn't. Smoking is a way to fill your life, and tonight it wasn't even worth trying to fool myself with such a hope.

Sunday. Another Sunday in the life of an invisible man. It sounds worse than it is; these twenty-four hours are normal and harmless to someone who doesn't cast a shadow. I could even say that I like these circumstances, that there are moments in them that I'm fond of, in which I recognize myself.

I haven't received any messages for days. The city is unchanged; I'm the same as ever. Just life. I watch vast quantities of ants crawling over the ground.

Clouds scud across the night sky. I've climbed on to the rooftop. Now and then a cool, humid breeze blows by ahead of the rain that will fall early tomorrow morning. Far off, the office buildings are almost completely dark.

Tomorrow will be the same, which is almost good news. I don't want to be somewhere else. That would be worse. It's too late now. This is what's left. This city is all I have.

My car's AC gave out. The streets smell again.

Days went by before an envelope appeared under the windshield wiper. I flattened out the sheet of unlined paper, which had been folded and refolded. Just above the center, in perfect miniscule handwriting (so, no slanted capital letters), was the message: "You haven't figured out anything. Calle Pointcaré. Grandma's Attic. Keep looking till you find me. S.W."

S.W.? Southwest? Some stranger's initials or the enigmatic Simone Weil once more? Pointcaré? I didn't recognize the street name, which sounded made-up, or maybe it was another hint. I had a vague memory of an art movement called *point carré*, but where? In France, Belgium, Switzerland?

I had to rifle through drawers and cabinets to find a map and scrutinize the metropolitan area. There were too many streets and the font was too small. I looked at the index and was surprised to find the street name from the note. It was near Avenida de Diego.

"Grandma's Attic." Was it a store? I had been in the area and knew it was mainly residential. There were office buildings, but I couldn't recall any shops other than restaurants.

I got into my car and was soon in El Condado. I decided to park and scope out the street on foot. There were houses and small apartment buildings. I walked past the street where the Alliance Française sits at the far end.

A bit farther along, I found an old wooden house with a tin roof. Over the door, a crudely lettered sign bore two words, in English: *Grandma's Attic*. The balcony was crammed with junk and old furniture. It was an antique store.

After crossing the threshold, I had to wait a few seconds for my eyes to adapt to the darkness. I discovered a series of rooms packed with all sorts of objects: furniture, dishes, crystal and ceramic knickknacks, musical instruments, table linens, picture frames. Behind a desk, a fat woman was talking on the phone in a blend of Spanish and English. She was obviously from the United States. As I walked by her, in the back of the store, I looked at her so inquiringly that she had to say hello.

I stayed in Grandma's Attic for about an hour, staring like an imbecile at trays full of silver spoons; old posters for festivals and conferences at the Institute of Puerto Rican Culture or the Interamerican University; souvenirs of Venice, Buenos Aires, or Washington; broken cameras; outdated maps; dozens of chairs with no seats hanging from the walls and the ceiling. I lost hope of finding a message in that welter of objects, the wreckage of lives that had nothing to do with my own.

One of the back rooms held books. I was led there by my love of reading and a sense that I had been wasting my time, but I could tell at a glance that hardly any of the books would be worthwhile. They were a mix of hardcover bestsellers from the United States, old encyclopedias that might have helped with someone's homework a couple of generations ago, a few classics that had undoubtedly passed through the hands of terrible teenage readers who had underlined whole pages and written their nicknames throughout the books, and Time Life manuals for plumbing or electrical wiring. Among these volumes that held no interest for me, I recognized the standard paperback binding of the French *Livre de Poche* series. There were two titles: a novel set in Italy by a woman whose name I did not recognize and a history of World War I. Both were practically ruined by the damp weather, the paper so deeply yellowed that the print was barely legible.

I was putting them back when my eye was drawn to the next shelf down, a hardcover book in English that had definitely not been on the bestseller list from ten or fifteen years ago. A translation of the biography of Simone Weil by Gabriella Fiori, it was also the only book I'd seen worth buying. Someone had read it, because several pages were marked up with neatly drawn lines, arrows, and asterisks. Some of the margins also had notes in a miniscule but equally careful hand. At the center of the book there was, as in most biographies, a photograph section printed on thick glossy paper. I looked through the photos one by one until I came across the image of Simone Weil with a cigarette in her hand sitting next to a man at a sidewalk café table. I was about to turn the page when I felt something: a note, taped to the back of the page. You could tell it hadn't been there long; the tape hadn't yellowed. Just above the center, written in a hand that I had seen for the first time just a couple of hours before, which I now realized was the same one in which all the marginal notes were written, were three short words: "You made it."

I closed the book, incapable of rereading the terse phrase, afraid that, if I were being watched, I would give away my discomposure. I wanted to phone someone right away, but Diego was traveling, and it was impossible to bring up the subject with Julia. I wished I could have something sure to hold onto and calm me down, some thought that would seem halfway appropriate, given the circumstances. The book was no secret, holding it in my hands was no cause for regret or shame, but for those moments I felt as if its touch burned.

I took it up to the desk where the woman sat. After glancing at it indifferently, she told me the price: three dollars. It was a bargain. Then she asked in English if I wanted anything else. I replied in Spanish, asking who had brought the book there. She didn't understand what I meant, even though she got all the words.

—Who brought you this book? I asked, switching to English.

—This book, she said, looking at it as if she might find a clue to the answer on the cover. Who knows! Lots of people bring in stuff. Some woman.

—*¿Cuándo?* I asked.

—A few times. She also buys stuff.

—*¿Cuándo lo trajo?* I asked again. When she gave you the book?

—Maybe a week ago. Give or take.

—You know her? You have her name? You keep a receipt? I am sorry, but it is important.

She must have thought I looked sufficiently decent, and the cardboard box with the receipts was sitting on the desk in front of her.

—*Vamos a ver*, she said, putting on her glasses. She peered over them at me, as if she were still trying to decide whether to give me the information. Then she flipped through slips of paper until she stopped.

—*Aquí está*. There she is. Simone Weil.

—*Ese es el título del libro*, I said.

—No, that's her name, said the woman.

—You're wrong. Look, it is the title, I said, jabbing my finger at the cover.

—No, it's her name. I don't write down the book titles. They don't matter to me. Just how many. See, three books. *Tres libros*. I remember now that she also brought two little French paperbacks. *Aquí está también su firma*, her signature, here. She writes very clearly: Simone Weil.

The woman showed me the receipt. She had signed it in the same handwriting used in the notes and the message from that morning. It had the precision of typewriting. She had brought three books, had gotten five dollars for them, had signed to leave a record of the agreement and for me to find her traces.

—I wonder why she didn't sign her real name, said the woman.

I, too, was wondering. Who was behind this game? At least now I knew it was a woman who had been writing to me for weeks in crude block letters that tilted toward the bottom of the paper, a handwriting she probably used only for that purpose, and that beginning today she was inscribing each word with the exactitude of a draftsman.

As soon as I got home, I opened Fiori's book and examined the marked-up pages. If they were somehow supposed to be messages addressed to me, I didn't understand anything. On page 64, however, a line and a half were underlined, and a tiny arrow pointed to a note: "Simone Weil was teaching philosophy to the railway workers at a night school on rue Falguière."

Could there still be any doubt? There has long since ceased to be any chance that this is a coincidence, a sick joke, or a hallucination. A woman is after me, but I don't know why, or who she is, or what she hopes to accomplish. A kind of fatalism makes me think I should expect the worst, but the situation starts to worry me when I admit to myself that I've willingly participated in this game of mirrors from the beginning; that Simone (can I really call her that now?), weaving her spider's web, has made me see that I haven't, in my whole life, done anything else; that this isn't the first time I've fallen in love with a faceless mask.

What about this is real? Here I am, looking at a book, reading and rereading every passage underlined by a woman whom I do not know yet am desperate to find. How is doing this different from the way I admire the façades of buildings I never enter or stare at women I find attractive, imagining their life stories? In the end it's just me, my mind, my legs, my car. I have such a capacity for traveling and gazing, for roaming the world weightlessly and leaving traces that fade and disappear. I think for a moment I could be different, and I have to hold tight to this possibility even if I'm wrong.

I've written an e-mail to Diego telling him what happened to me. He is as intelligent as he is insensitive. Just one line on the computer screen, not even hello or good-bye or anything: "'A man can't be angry at his own era without suffering some damage,' Robert Musil."

At first it bothered me. I felt this was no time to cite literature, though I had to admit his choice of a quotation was almost as good as Simone's. I mulled over my dissatisfaction for half the morning before concluding that Diego, in his own way, was playing the same game. This ability not to take ourselves seriously was what had drawn us together from the time we met, and now, it served to put things in perspective for me. In the end I was grateful to him. Maybe I had shown the messages too much respect. More than likely, I was taking the whole thing too seriously.

Even so, half an hour later, I was back at Grandma's Attic. When I went up to her desk, I could tell that the owner was watching me with concern.

—She hasn't come, she said before I could ask anything.

—That doesn't matter. But when she does come in, give her this.

—Should I say anything else?

—*No hace falta*. Just give her the envelope.

—Are you guys in love?

—*Sí, mucho*, I answered.

Even before I turned thirty, I knew that what I most wanted was to put my life into a book. I suffered so I could write my suffering. That way life had direction; that way alone it was worth squeezing life to the last drop, here or anywhere else. This set me apart from almost everyone. But I didn't mind because I was discovering and rediscovering who I was, and I asked for nothing else. The shadow that had crisscrossed the city for years and years wasn't a man passing through a transitory bad phase he'd get over someday. No, not even close, though I had always assumed this was true. I had been waiting for a change, a trip, a new job, or even exile. Without realizing it, I had already found my place. This was what I should be, this man I so despised was the person I wanted to resemble.

More than two weeks went by without any news, but this silence was different. The search had taken on a different tone since I had given the envelope to the owner of Grandma's Attic and since I had announced with breathtaking certainty that I loved a woman I didn't know. It was obviously a huge risk to take, but I knew that avoiding risks and being sensible is sometimes the craziest thing you can do.

Inside the envelope I'd copied the phrase that Rodrigo de Figueroa wrote on the map of San Juan Islet, drawn on his orders in 1509 when they were considering transferring the capital from Caparra, "Here shall the city be," repeating the phrase below with a short addition: "If you wish, here shall the city be, without question." Later on, doubts and questions would assail me, but at the time, it was the most honest declaration of love I had ever made. The messages I had received deserved an answer. One of the most apt images of a love story is the streets of the city that gave birth to and in time may witness the death of that love.

The Chinese restaurant on Avenida Muñoz Rivera had a sign posted next to the cash register: "Try our delicious flan! We have ice cream!" The sign didn't look any more Chinese than the Dominican woman who almost always took the orders. A little after the regular dinnertime, I would sit, once or twice a week, at one of the tables in the nearly empty dining room, and if I didn't open my notebook to jot something down, I would sit looking through the service window into the kitchen, watching the hustle and bustle of the cooks, in their case authentically Chinese. Sometimes women were back there, or maybe a little girl learning to count in Spanish (*"¡Uno, dos, tres, cinco!"*), members of what was probably an extended family that lived somewhere in the building.

Only rarely did anyone enter the place at that hour, maybe a couple of policemen or a friend of the Dominican woman, who would while away the time by standing at the long mirrored wall and popping her pimples. The food was awful and more than once I spotted insects crawling on the counter. Even so, I kept coming back. When I was there, out of the house, far from everything, even from myself, I was at peace, and feeling at home in such a dreary atmosphere was also a way of transcending it.

One night, after eating a plate of fried rice, I opened the Simone Weil biography I had bought in Grandma's Attic. I sat reading it for nearly an hour, and the Chinese cooks started giving me distrusting looks. It was unusual for someone to stay there that long.

The restaurant was connected to a sushi bar that I had never gone into. Both must have had the same owner, who was thus able to offer menus for every pocketbook. A waitress came in through the door connecting the two places and asked the Dominican woman to make change. I realized that they were looking at me, that the waitress was staring at my things: the notes, the book. Soon afterward she came back in, but then they called her from the other restaurant. Later she entered for a third time, and this time she went straight to my table. I knew she was approaching me, but I waited until her black-stockinged legs stood planted in front of me before I lifted my eyes from the book.

—Do you like Simone Weil? she asked.

Coming from an unknown waitress in that restaurant, this felt like one of the most disconcerting questions I'd ever heard.

—I'm starting to, I said.

—Here. I study at the university and I've seen you there. Maybe we can talk about Simone Weil someday. I work next door, but now I have to go.

—Thanks, I said, taking the small brown paper bag she handed me. Before she turned her back on me to go, for a brief instant, we looked eye to eye. We had spoken without saying a word. Then I watched her until she disappeared behind the door that divided the two restaurants. She must have been about twenty-five, though it was hard to tell for sure.

I opened the bag with trembling hands, amazed, but already confident. It held a sheet of paper, folded as usual, and a fortune cookie. I set them on the table and looked around. The Dominican woman was on the phone, but she seemed to be waiting to see what I'd do. The Chinese cooks were bustling around the kitchen, indifferent. I unfolded the paper. Just above the center, in a miniscule and near-perfect hand, was a quotation. This time I could be sure because for the first time the author's name was provided:

"Freedom is not a human right conferred by Heaven. Nor does the freedom to dream come at birth: it is a capacity and an awareness that needs to be defended. Moreover, even dreams can be assailed by nightmares.—Gao Xinjian, *One Man's Bible*"

I picked up the fortune cookie and broke it in half. There was the usual strip of paper inside, but this time the printed message had been crossed out. On the back was written, in the same handwriting as the quotation, "Page 46." I knew it referred to the book I had there on the table, the book that had brought us to this same part of the city.

On that page was an underlined passage, with an arrow pointing to it from the margin:

"Beyond all schemes, she lives in what will be more and more a contact between souls. She is unaware of the carnal character of daily life as she is of the conventions and rites of social classes; thus, even on the social plane, Simone Weil will be perceived as inhuman."

I gathered my things and went outside. I walked by the darkened windows of the sushi bar. Inside the light was dim, but I thought I could see a silhouette following me with her eyes. I stopped and put my hand on my chest, over my heart. I felt I could see her do the same.

The following day I found this message on my answering machine:

"Hello, I'm Li Chao, alias Simone Weil. I think it's time I introduced myself. I hope you'll forgive my little game (I suppose I can speak informally now). As you must have noticed, I take it very seriously, though I know it could cause trouble. I may not be able to see you, sir, umm, I mean, I can't see you till Thursday, my day off. I suggest we meet at the Starbucks on San Patricio. I'm not as mysterious as you must suppose. I said hello to you there a long time ago, but you didn't realize I was the woman leaving the messages. And there's no reason why you should have. We can meet at the same time as before—that is, at 7:49 p.m. You don't have to show up, of course. Ciao from Li Chao."

I left the message on the machine and listened to it many more times over the following days. I had felt in control of my life, though at times it seemed utterly worthless. Li Chao had demolished what was, I discovered, an ineffective defense mechanism. Life was an uncontrollable torrent. I had long observed it comfortably, from the banks; now, I was captive to its unpredictability.

The citadel had fallen. I wondered if, after Thursday night, I'd be a different person. I could never have anticipated someone using these texts or this strategy to get close to me. I was so limited. Li Chao was coming from another direction.

I counted the days and hours and at the same time wished Thursday night would never come. I had fallen in love with the tactical brilliance of an approach that had turned into something like a work of art. I wasn't stupid or naïve enough to think that what I now imagined was desirable or even possible. But at the same time, I was convinced there was a crack in my defenses: Li Chao's messages were a kind of secret tunnel I had just uncovered. There was a way past the walls I had always raised around myself.

The Starbucks server took my order and handed me a folded note. It was handwritten in the second style, the maniacally precise one. "It was an ancient beauty, like an old photograph set afire." There was an asterisk sending me to another phrase at the bottom of the page. "I wait for you where you have gone so often." I was going to ask the girl serving me where the woman who'd given her the note was, when I suddenly got an idea.

—Be right back, I said while paying, and I ran over to Castle Books, literally a step away.

I went to the literature section, but no one was there. I entered the next aisle, with four bookshelves of Puerto Rican books. I had noticed a few days earlier that they had put one of mine on the top shelf. But now the transparent plastic stand where *Three-in-One* had been was empty.

Unsuccessful, very nervous, I searched the whole bookstore. Then I went out into the mall. Li wasn't in the restaurant area or standing by the movie theater. I returned and again walked through each aisle in the bookstore.

Only the children's section, which was separated by a wall from the rest of the store, remained to be searched. When I entered, Li Chao was reading my book, sitting on a chair in the shape of an elephant.

—You know how to get where you're going, she said, barely raising her eyes. You do it well, she added.

It wasn't clear whether she was talking about my finding her or about my book.

—You too, I said. Too well.

—I hope you'll forgive me for the complications.

—For you, picking up a phone and dialing is too old-fashioned.

—If I'd done that, you wouldn't have come.

For the first time, we saw each other face to face, without the screen of messages between us. It was so easy; it seemed unreal to me. I got the feeling that something was missing, that some basic piece was absent, yet her body was in front of me.

—Come on, let's get a coffee, I said.

—You'll have to buy. Starbucks is too expensive.

I observed her, walking through the mall. For the first time, I could look at her by my side. Before, for many weeks, I was the one who had been examined at will. I was now finding out about the body of this woman, medium in height, dressed in a T-shirt and a pair of wide pants that she hardly filled. She had a shoulder bag, probably woven somewhere in Central America, and almost hidden under the large bells of the pant legs, a pair of plastic sandals.

After so much excitement, this body was almost a disappointment. However, I was sure that if it had been any other I would have thought the same. From the messages, I had constructed a phenomenon in my head that blew reality out of proportion. No beauty could have compared, at least not at first blush, with that fantasy.

Before we sat down, Li picked up a chess set and brought it to our table.

—I'll be white, she said, and I realized that behind the grammatical perfection of her words lay an unusual intonation, a peculiar way to attack certain sounds.

—Of course, you always like to keep one step ahead.

After a few moves, I'd lost three pieces, and when I hesitated for a long time over whether to move a bishop, I heard her say,

—Every four seconds a child dies of hunger somewhere on the planet.

She must have seen that I didn't understand because she added impatiently,

—At least two hundred have died by now.

That was Li. She seemed to know all the statistics in the world, the illuminating ones and the trivial ones alike. She knew the per capita income of Togo, the inflation rate in Peru, how many more years the tropical forests of the world had left at the current rate of clear-cutting, the number of automobiles in Puerto Rico, and as a point of comparison, the number in Sudan; she knew how many pints of blood the human body contained and the weight of dolphins' brains, how many spermatozoa there were in an ejaculation, and how many kilos of salmon a bear ate during an Alaskan spring.

When she referenced a set of numbers at inappropriate times, it was like she was parodying the way we cite facts, questioning through exaggeration the numerical reality of the world. I observed her strong hands; the slight plumpness of her body that she tried to hide with loose clothes; her round face with full, pale cheeks; her black, listless hair parted in the middle and frequently tied back in pigtails. Taken all together, I realized, she would lead me to surprises. Li, a Chinese woman living on a Caribbean island who approached the works of novelists, thinkers, and artists as if they were musical scores to be interpreted, took every aspect of life like a young girl who'd seen it all.

I watched as she drank two café con leches, ate three different kinds of pastry, let me win our very quick, second chess game.

I remembered the passages she had underlined in the Simone Weil biography. Almost all of them established the distance at which the thinker had lived from her contemporaries, even if she had been so committed to those in need that she had attempted to repair that separation. More than one heartache lay behind her dedication. I'd seen enough of Li, though we'd never met in person before this night, that I could imagine her reasons for choosing her pseudonym.

—Why Simone Weil? I asked.

—I like that name. She used to study on her knees.

—On her knees?

—Yes, she studied on her knees, spent hours reading on her knees. She was a philosopher who had been humbled. She was half crazy but totally lucid. What I respect most about her work is that she understood that you don't stop being humbled after you learn that's who you are. She never claimed to escape that reality.

—Why me? I asked. Where did you see me, how did you find out about me, why all this effort, this game that you took so seriously?

—I met you through your books, and then I saw you at the university. I'm the only Chinese woman in comparative literature.

—You know you're not answering the question.

—Of course.

—So?

—It's impossible, or rather it would be complicated, to give you an answer tonight. The important thing is that we've gotten this far, and I really thank you for coming. Aside from that, you can use this opportunity to improve your chess game.

Starbucks was closing, and Li went to the bathroom. A short time later the server brought me a note. "They're coming to pick me up. If you'd like, you can stop by the restaurant. I get off at 10:30. Don't obsess about the whys. Over the long run, I know that nothing can stay hidden. Ciao. Li"

As the weeks went by, I would realize the extent to which Li lived in a practically closed world, still untouched by the consumer society or basic liberties, where high status meant having a tiny room of your own to sleep in, with space in a corner for storing your clothes and, in Li's case, for keeping a few piles of books and papers.

She worked six days a week in the restaurant and had done so from the age of eleven. She was a distant relative of the family that owned a half dozen Chinese food places in San Juan and in a few towns on the island. She had been born in 1969 in a small village on the outskirts of Beijing that was, according to Li, an unhealthy flatland, cold and damp, full during that era of officials forced by the Cultural Revolution to be "reeducated" through agricultural labor. She held onto few memories: the muddy pools that filled the streets, the endless rice fields, the taste of boiled potatoes, her grandmother's lap, a couple of songs. Her family had to split up because her father, a math teacher, was accused of coming from a family of "intellectuals." Given the abject human relationships imposed by the Cultural Revolution, this meant that Li's mother could not maintain any ties to her husband, and she was forced to denounce him and repudiate him formally and publicly. Her father was sent to villages farther and farther away from the capital until he must have succumbed to the cold, the hunger, the sentence he had been given for knowing how to read and write, for owning Soviet geometry textbooks and an old prerevolutionary translation of *Madame Bovary*, for having a bourgeois taste for jazz. After countless close calls, her mother managed to reach Hong Kong with Li, and from there, of all the places in the world, they traveled to Puerto Rico thanks to the efforts of some distant family members. She was six when she arrived.

Early on she didn't even live in San Juan; she shared an apartment with other family members on the second story built with unfinished concrete blocks above the Gran Muralla restaurant in Arecibo. From there, she'd moved to one on Avenida Fernández Juncos in Santurce. At school and on the street, she was always *la china*. For years, hardly anyone outside the restaurant called her by her name. Nobody was interested or could understand her history. The distance, size, and complexity of China made it unfathomably abstract.

She lived with cousins, aunts, uncles, and "relatives" of unknown kinship, in grotesque overcrowding. She was the only one who learned how to speak and read Spanish well, and this was probably why they let her graduate from a public school in Santurce. There she was one of the few students who got to the last pages of books and the only one who spent all her free time in the modest library.

After a long struggle, she managed to persuade her family and, at the age of twenty, she enrolled in the Universidad de Puerto Rico. She somehow found a way to put herself through college, and in particular to pay her full tuition, by working at the restaurant. She submitted to unwritten rules: the restaurant owner's family had gotten her out of China, and it was her obligation to work for him in exchange for a roof over her head and laughable wages over an indefinite period that might last her whole life. Now, Li said, she was working to purchase her freedom in the family's best restaurant, the one where you earned the most. Apart from her fellow students, who always kept their distance from her, I was the first non-Chinese man she had taken the initiative to get to know.

After giving me this sparse outline of her life, she said I could now understand why she preferred books to men and why, of all possible men, she had felt curious about a man who was a writer.

—Hardly anybody reads me, I said.

—Hardly anybody sees me, Li replied, or if they see me, they see a Chinese woman. Not many can see anything more.

—We're alike. Why don't you write?

—Do you read Chinese?

—You could write in Spanish, you speak it so well.

—I couldn't do it in Chinese either. I never learned to write in Chinese, and I speak it like an immigrant. I can say, "You rike big prate flied lice." My problem isn't the language but the impossibility everyone else has of imagining me. Is it possible to write when no one shares your identity, when the vast majority of people can't even imagine you?

—Do you think it's so different for me? Besides, I added, that can be a good literary space. Isn't a writer already a species apart?

—But being a Chinese woman in Puerto Rico is much more extreme.

—That's natural. It's hard anywhere to be a writer, even harder to get yourself read with a minimum of attention. Your position here is extreme, but that's not enough to convince me. There's something else.

—You can't write if you have no words, said Li. If the words have always belonged to others. That's why I prefer to read, to take the words that others write and transform them. That's what I'm familiar with. That's what I've always done.

—Then it's what you should do, I said.

—It's what I did with you.

I'd go see her at ten, when few diners remained in the restaurant and the employees wrapping up their shifts were straightening the tables and leaving the place ready for the next day. We rarely talked in her room. I'd invite her to a pizza place or a restaurant with Puerto Rican cuisine; either way, she loved the food. I came to see from the way she ate that Li had never taken food for granted. She chewed conscientiously, with perfect concentration, and didn't leave a bite on her plate.

—Do you remember China, from when you were a child?

—Of course. But my memory has more gaps than anything. I don't remember the past so much as *feel* it. Maybe that's hard to see, but for me, it's been normal. The past is something I find in silence. I've spent my life surrounded by noise, first in China with my family and the neighbors who practically lived with us, then in Hong Kong among the refugees, later on in Arecibo, in San Juan, in the noisy racket of the kitchens and the traffic of the avenues reaching the rooms where I've lived day and night, but my life has been coming and going, if I can put it like this, to silence.

—Does it bother you?

—I've had no other option. This is the only world I've been

in. The world of Li Chao; the planet whose total population is made up only of me: one Chinese woman among more than a billion Chinese, one Chinese woman on an island where there are no Chinese except in restaurants, one Chinese woman who doodles and reads.

After midnight, I'd drop her off in front of the restaurant. She lived in the rooftop apartment. Then I'd go home, which wasn't far. It was the coolest part of the day and I felt fine. Things were better since Li was there.

I wouldn't go straight to sleep. I'd put on music. Drink a glass of juice. Look for a notebook and write. For the first time in a long while I was content.

I'd get into bed and contemplate the shadows the trees made on the ceiling. I didn't even know whether I wanted to sleep with Li, whether there was any need.

A couple of times I tried to get her out of her regular environment. She had been living in this country for more than twenty years and had hardly been outside of San Juan and Arecibo, the city on the north coast where she'd spent part of her childhood. It was difficult to believe, but she'd hardly ever gone swimming in the sea.

I took advantage of some of her Thursdays off to take her to Salinas or Cabo Rojo and eat fresh fish or to introduce her to a beach or a forest. I met with little success, as there were few people more urban than Li. For her, nature was to be found in a can of bamboo shoots or a large sack of rice. All the rest was a bad memory or something she had no intention of experiencing. She therefore preferred to go on short excursions where, instead of doing anything I might suggest, we'd wander around the city on foot or by car till very late, on more than one occasion getting to watch the sunrise from the sea shore in a park in El Condado.

We'd talk for hours, drinking a thermos of tea from the same cup, spinning the stories of our lives and of the books we'd read. For someone like her, culture wasn't about privileges or entertainment. Instead, as she stole time from her sleep and work and put up with the incomprehension of those around her, she was using culture as a weapon for survival.

As the sun was rising, I'd rush her back to the restaurant, before the city's avenues and express lanes became clogged with traffic. Li would sleep a few hours, work her shift, read in the afternoon if there were no diners in the restaurant, and wait for me to arrive every night.

During the day, I'd recall how she would speak with her face turned aside, eyes fixed on the horizon. I'd remember the stories she told in the nearly flawless Spanish that had earned her a promotion to waitress in the clan's best restaurant and permitted her the rebellious act of going to college. Though an enormous gulf separated our origins, in the intonations of her voice and the stories behind them, I heard the deep rumbling of the city that had befallen us like a sickness.

On one occasion, Li had to sub for a fellow worker on a Thursday, so she got a rare Friday off.

—I'd like to show you something I've been working on, she told me over the phone. Take me out somewhere. Indoors, please.

—You want to have pizza, I suggested, knowing how much she liked it.

Friday night had just begun and a river of cars was slowly flowing out to the suburbs and shopping centers along Avenida Muñoz Rivera. When I got to the sushi bar, Li had been waiting on the corner for a while. She had her hair in a ponytail and wore a black skirt and a pale, vaguely Asian blouse. She carried her usual cloth bag on her shoulder.

I brought some bad news. I'd learned that afternoon that the editors of an anthology had decided to cut me from the project. I should have been brave enough to admit that there had always been a chance of my being cut, so I had nothing to gain from acting moody or listless. Still, I was irritated when they used the clumsy excuse of my books' publication dates to justify excluding me. More likely they hadn't even read my stuff. Once more, they'd rely on personal whims and the old boy's network to bestow recognition. It wasn't much of a consolation for me that Máximo Noreña was also spurned. In his case, the editors' reasons had been even more awkward and baseless.

Creeping toward El Condado, trapped in traffic among hundreds of other cars, I found it hard to react to the enthusiasm with which Li was weaving her sentences. The bad news kept spinning in my mind and I couldn't turn it off.

Streets and avenues were gridlocked, and there was no way to reach the highway entrance ramps. It took us more than half an hour to reach Santurce, and it was uncertain whether we could continue to El Condado on Avenida de Diego because of a concert being held in Bellas Artes. I remembered a pizzeria nearby where I'd eaten with Diego. A *lucha libre* star I'd seen on TV as a child used to hang out there. His forehead, much darker than the rest of his face, was covered by a scar that looked like tree bark.

I parked in front of an exquisite house, probably built in the 1930s, that had been abandoned for years and was up for sale. We walked one block to the pizzeria, full of families and couples, and sat down in the only free booth.

I tried using the noise level inside the place as a cover for my silence. I hardly ate, letting Li devour the anchovy pizza. To talk about something, trying to disguise my reticence, I told her about the wrestler who used to be a regular at the restaurant. I was surprised to learn she knew perfectly well who I was talking about. For the Chinese who barely understood Spanish (also true of her at the time), *The Stars of Lucha Libre* was one of the few programs they could follow. The twenty inhabitants of the rooftop apartment would sit down in front of the TV set every Saturday, with a passion comparable only to what they felt watching martial arts films from Hong Kong.

Li knew what was going on with me since I had told her about it on the slow drive to the restaurant. I supposed my bad mood would dry up like a puddle, leaving a dry, brittle scab like the wrestler's forehead. That's how I was treating Li's first Friday off, overwhelmed by negativity, no desire to do anything.

—Here, she said. It's for you.

She had pulled from her bag a roll of paper no more than eight inches wide. I took it and started unrolling it. I soon realized it would be almost impossible to finish the job there since it was more than six feet long.

—I used up three ballpoint pens making it, she said when she saw in my face that my mood had lifted.

From top to bottom, except for the narrow natural margins, Li had covered the long sheet in one labyrinthine line, creating a black mass that looked alive, as if it might be vibrating a millimeter above the surface. It was an epic feat of determination and patience, both the tireless cycling of a machine and the unique mark of a hand.

—Do you like it? she asked.

—It's the best thing I've seen in a long time.

I wasn't lying. Her drawing stood out against the works of many artists that were nothing but parodies of international fashions.

—But it's ridiculous, she said. Three ballpoint pens' worth of ink, on two meters of the paper that comes on rolls for the restrooms in the restaurant, drawn by a Chinese woman with no title who works like a dog in a country where *chinitos* aren't supposed to be good for anything but selling egg drop soup and egg rolls. In other words, the work of a nobody. I suppose I ought to do like you, spoil the night and cry in a corner.

—But it's so good, I said. You should use better paper. And not ballpoints.

—That wouldn't change anything. It would even reduce its impact. You don't realize, you're looking at an anonymous work. Li Chao doesn't exist. She's just one Chinese woman from among 1,300,000,000 Chinese, not counting those who've emigrated and are living overseas, and from among 4,000,000 Puerto Ricans who don't even look at themselves. A lesbian who took to using the words of others to pursue a writer whose failure is eating away at him today.

She rarely talked about herself. Her efforts to contact me had been a very effective way to avoid confessions. She armored herself in other people's words and, at the same time, used them to express herself elliptically. Her lesbianism didn't come as a surprise, but her decision to tell me about it did. She was trying to draw me out of my shell and force me to see her. She didn't want our relationship to be a failure. Neither did I. I wanted something from her, and despite her confession, I felt I wasn't far away.

I took her hand, and we gazed eye to eye until we both looked down at the same moment. A man and a woman are transformed when they look straight at each other and for the first time the silence doesn't weigh on them. After that they'd be fooling themselves if they pretended nothing was going to happen. A new story begins then, and there's no backing away.

I asked for the check.

—I want to show you something now, I said.

The avenues had freed up. I went down Ponce de León to the bridge that connected with the islet of San Juan, turned around, and drove to San Patricio. We felt a peace and calm in the confines of the car that we hadn't shared till then.

In front of the shopping center where we had first met, I made a U-turn and took Avenida Kennedy toward San Juan. On a Friday at that hour, in this area lined by dealerships where they sold every model of car on the country's roads, there wasn't a soul to be seen. As I held the gear shift, Li rested her hand on mine and brought her head close until it rested on my shoulder. I turned toward her and, for a second, held the warmth of her lips on mine.

—Now look at the lights on the bridge, I said.

We looked ahead at the streetlight poles. Constitution Bridge was a kilometer and a half away. Crossing it, we would have Hato Rey on our right and on our left San Juan Bay. I was going exactly fifty miles an hour. I had it all calculated: I had done it countless times. The streetlight poles created the illusion of rising up until, for a few seconds, with the magical precision of optical illusions they formed two gigantic question marks on either side of the avenue. Realizing what she saw, Li squeezed my hand, and I heard her speak so close that her voice seemed to be coming from inside me.

—I'm sorry. I must have filled your head with questions. If it's any consolation to you, you don't know how many questions you've raised for me.

—Tonight is full of the hardest questions.

—I know, and perhaps they have no answers.

A little later, we were back in Santurce and once again were driving along sections of Avenida Ponce de León. The city seemed to constrict us with its limited circuits. It wasn't worth repeating the same trip. Undecided and fearful, I asked:

—What do you want to do?

I felt her search for the answer, hold it in her mind for a second, and dare to say it.

—Take me to your place. All I ask you is not to penetrate me.

I had never made love under such a severe restriction, but as in so many other things, Li led me through unexplored territory. Her full breasts, the graceful curve of her belly, the skin of her shoulders, which seemed covered by a film of wax, the matchless warmth and skill of her tongue, her ability to be present even in the slightest movements, made it so that the impossibility of consummating the act forced me to discover the delights of holding back.

The prohibition heightened our yearning. Our sessions were oblivious of time, lacking an obvious ending. Our movements stretched out endlessly and effortlessly. The act was unfulfillable, at least it was for me, and the energy traveled through my body without ever running out. In joining our bodies, we were creating an uncharted territory where past experience was no guide, and the wide field before us defied all assumptions. It was impossible to know what we'd find in it and what was expected of us.

The loneliness and suffering that had accumulated for years, the weight of an entire lifetime, had brought us here. We were castaways sharing a single raft in the ocean of San Juan's streets and it was clear that if we hadn't been so deprived we would never have met. What we were doing, to be honest, was unworkable. In the impossible place where we were making love like cripples, we were blind people at the edge of an abyss. We would fall on each other, biting, sliding tongues over nipples and navels, obsessed with slowly examining the forbidden orifice, observing it, circling it, tensing it, without blinking, without looking away. We surrendered to each other with no rules but the one we were testing, discovering our next movement only at the moment of making it. Her breasts struck against my chest, I grabbed her arms tight, pulled on her ponytail, then went down again to her groin until the irresistible power of a great wave made her arch her back again and again. We would go on without resting and throw ourselves upon each other, wordlessly, sometimes looking at one another with a gaze harder than an erect member, and more memorable. After hours, when we were on the verge of collapse, Li would take me in her mouth, with the total devotion that she reserved for her drawings, until a graceful and solemn overspilling came almost from beyond my body. My semen would fall, sprinkling on lips and neck and then running down to the belly or dripping from her chin like a teardrop, dense and enormous.

Then, arms and legs entwined, our bodies would begin to come back to life: we'd rediscover that our limbs were each our own and that they marked the difference and distance between us. There was no need for a concrete event to come along and undo us. It had already happened; not in the history we were making, but in what came before us. Since Li lost her father; since she crossed half a world and came here; since I resolved to survive, disgusted with everything but clinging to my disgust; since we began, we were condemned to fail.

Silence would descend upon us like a membrane, solidifying until it undid our embrace. We'd remain beside each other for a while, in growing and indefinable unease. Our thoughts lingered on the sweat-dampened sheets, the semen crystalizing on skin, the hunger, the thirst, or the embarrassment of a newfound modesty. The battle to build a citadel with our two bodies, to find some answer or security, was over. Li would stand up and disappear into the shower without saying a word, eager to erase the marks of our relations with soap and water. I would watch her clumsily cross the room, getting tangled up in shoes and pieces of clothing tossed to the floor, and my spirit would quickly go from tenderness to something that could be called many things and that was nothing but affliction. It was a hard, stubborn grief I had known since I was first aware of time, of loneliness, and of grief itself.

Li had conquered me with the brilliance of her messages, and she didn't conceal from me that behind them lurked an ambition of control. A lesbian had fallen in love with a man, and he returned her love, but she was the one who decided on the rules of the game. I wasn't happy with the role I'd been assigned, and the prohibition seemed a constant threat. I had never imagined keeping up a relationship of this nature. If I had ventured to try, it was because Li was a mystery. I didn't know, beyond the obvious reasons (and even those were not all that obvious), why she had sought me out, why she had confronted herself and confronted me with a love (is that what it really was, or was I completely deceived?) that might at any moment prove impossible. Where was Li's body and where was mine when I was with her? Didn't I have the absurd absence of her body before me, a distance that would forever be unbridgeable and incomprehensible? Could I live with a woman with whom, as I traveled toward her, I always lost myself?

Li would emerge from the shower without looking at me, combing her fingers through her well-drenched hair with overly studied slowness. She would climb into bed and run her fingers through lock after lock, repeating the same gesture over and over without a break. When she felt my hand, she would seek my eyes. Invariably, after we had made love, in her eyes I saw fear.

A few minutes later, when after getting up and showering I was getting dressed in the bedroom, I would watch her sitting with her knees raised and her back against the headboard, lost in thought, still combing her hair. Then I'd ask her if she felt well, watch her tilt her head and nod, while her hair, falling like a curtain across her face, prevented me from knowing whether it were true.

I tried to spend as much time with her as possible. I went to the restaurant when her shift ended and often joined the employees for dinner there. As time went on, the boss, the entrepreneurial patriarch of the family for whom Li, bound by some shady debt, was forced to work, came to accept my nearly daily presence. He took the initiative to consult with me about some matter in the hopes that my belonging to San Juan society would open up some commercial opportunity for him or provide profitable relationships. In the long run, he realized that I wouldn't be able to help him, and he took me for one more of his "niece's" eccentricities.

In this way, I joined in many late suppers at the table in the back of the restaurant where the employees ate after a long day's work. Li's relatives and fellow workers, free at last, stopped and sat down, shouted their conversations, disregarding all decorum and respect, in a relaxed revelry where exhaustion briefly intermingled with euphoria. Those suppers, without tact or affection, were the result of years during which they had put up with each other practically every hour of every day, in the narrow quarters of kitchens, dining rooms, and sleeping rooms that had turned them into not a family so much as a community stranded in a strange land. Being with them brought to mind the people who ate at fixed times on the benches of a boarding school or a barracks.

I realized that they were sometimes talking about us at the table, being brazenly insolent toward Li, who understood what they were saying. I didn't know whether they envied her for having gotten her hands on a partner from outside their circle, or whether they did it simply as an expression of boredom or cruelty. According to Li, not eating with them would have been worse. She had to see their faces every day, and she couldn't quit her job. Being independent of it all was for the moment impossible.

These people, the father of the current owner of the restaurant, had put up the money to bring her and her mother from China. They had given her food and shelter. This had established an obligation, and not a merely financial one, that she couldn't just wash her hands of.

After several weeks, as the strength of our bond grew evident, Li's "family" ceased to care whether she spent the night with me. She seemed to feel comfortable in my house, making herself at home, taking whatever she wanted, books, this piece of clothing or that, bustling about the kitchen as much as she pleased, but it occurs to me now that she never asked for anything: neither a drawer for her things nor a desk to draw at. Nor did she indicate any preferences: one side of the bed, one type of food, one product brand. That likely had to do with her habit of practically living on borrowed things, sharing everything with others, and owning nothing but a few objects, but perhaps it was also a way of being prepared for an eventuality that she knew was, despite it all, always lying in wait. From the time she left her village on the outskirts of Beijing, she'd had nothing to hold onto but the community of Chinese with whom she worked. She lived as lightly as possible. The only thing tying her down was a debt and the impossibility of leaving this country. In both cases, it was a question of chains.

One thing, however, was always clear: I couldn't force or impose anything on her. Persistent questions would always put her in a dark and taciturn mood. I'd have to suggest a topic or a concern and get a strictly factual explanation hours or even days later. This was clearly an overreaction, a defensive move, but she was incapable of dealing with some areas of her life in any other way. Sometimes I felt Li lived on a narrow ridge of land beside a deep gorge. There was very little room to maneuver.

Those were the conditions; I could take them or leave them. She never told me so openly, but it was always obvious. Her situation and sexual preferences had not been a mystery. In fact, I had suspected them, and she made matters clear from the beginning.

Nevertheless, she alone set the limits. So long as we were together, she enjoyed a freedom that I never had.

These uncertainties and shades of gray, contrary to what might be supposed, increased our desire to be together. It was as if we imagined the end was already living with us and that we had to struggle to delay it. Our desire grew when we realized it was mortally wounded, and in bed, we would dive into a tidal wave where we hardly sensed our own silhouettes. Even so, our fears were never far away.

From the depths of that ocean, we would surface to talk about books and authors, about performance art, about Duchamp, John Cage, and Diogenes of Sinope, creating an island of shared passions on the other island that was a daily affront to who we were. When we went outside some people stopped to stare. We were hardly a circus act, but I'm sure that they sensed our strangeness. In this way we negotiated, at times with indifference and at times with pride, the rapids of a society where we had always felt unwanted. Even so, life was better, indubitably better, since Li was there.

At the university, Li had enrolled as a comparative literature student, but she had also taken courses in many other departments. Her interests were extremely broad, and she could read Foucault or an FAO report with equal interest. She had, as her messages revealed, a vast and idiosyncratic command of literature, even more admirable when you learned that, unable to afford these books, she had read them all standing in bookstores over the course of many days. Taking her origins and circumstances into account, it was a miracle she had become the woman she now was. She worked as a waitress all day long, but at lunch and during her free time, she consumed an impressive number of pages. When she discussed them with me, she demonstrated a deep and original understanding. What fell into her hands seemed to reassemble itself, and someone else's text ended up being, through her reading, a redefined text that shone brightly. She was always busy, usually reading and drawing; she only rested when she slept. In her waking life, there couldn't be any empty space, a moment for fantasy or idleness. She struggled to make the best use of every hour, every minute, all day long.

On some occasions, we would sit to watch a movie, but after a short time I would see her taking out her notebook and drawing without looking up.

—You never rest, I would say.

—I've never been able to, she'd answer.

—You aren't watching the movie.

—Of course I am, she would reply with a touch of pride. I'm drawing from the movie. If I weren't watching it, I wouldn't be drawing this.

As time passed by, the blotches of black ink from her drawings grew and multiplied. She dropped the small-format notebooks and used progressively larger sheets of paper, which she kept in a portfolio case that I gladly gave her as a present, for which she was as grateful as a child. Her works invaded her room in the rooftop apartment at the restaurant, my house, and even, with one sublime piece, the horrid wall of my university office.

It was an elegantly crafted work. Successive rows of ink plowed across the paper's surface to create areas of deep intensity. If the strokes had been drawn in a straight line, Li's hand would have covered countless meters, but here her effort was concentrated on a few square centimeters. The lines erased their passage until they became a solid, pulsing body that took a mammoth feat of tedious and hypnotic labor. In the end, there was seemingly nothing or nearly nothing on the paper: a more or less purely geometric form with slight glimmers of white, the minimal patches of paper not covered by the tip of the pen. The result was austere and bedazzling and also constituted a powerful conceptual design. Rather than an erased drawing, like the famous de Kooning that Rauschenberg had painstakingly "erased," Li's drawing disappeared under the excess that seemed to penetrate the paper and, at the same time, to float above it. It was a nearly infinite series of strokes, and it was impossible to tell where or when they ended. She wasn't interested in finding out, it was enough for her that it remained alive, covering its tracks, turning the finest line into the densest shading, the most insurmountable wall.

Progressively my enthusiasm grew greater. I had seen little art in recent years that aroused my enthusiasm. It would be easy to think I was blinded by love and all the associated clichés, but in the case of her drawings, quite apart from the desire that your beloved should be extraordinary, there was the brute fact of a body of work being created with equal discipline in all sorts of places and circumstances. Li carried her notebooks and rolls of paper with her and, indifferent to her surroundings, she got down to work. She only stopped when her stiff, cramped hand could not keep going.

Once, I told her she was a Penelope who, instead of undoing the shroud nightly, was constructing one so vast and dense it could never be completed. My comment was meant to be light, and I couldn't have imagined the enigma contained in her reply. "Whether I wish it or not, I am waiting too," she said, and kept on drawing, protecting herself with a silence I didn't have the courage to break.

My interest in art was reborn, and we glimpsed the possibility of doing projects together. Little by little our relationship turned into a working one. The process of my hunting, the pursuit Li had carried out through her messages, already constituted a sort of conceptualism, with the added merit of having erased the border between art and life, which after all had been the desire of so many vanguard artists.

An enigmatic and unprecedented Chinese–Puerto Rican was creating, without pretensions of any kind, almost spontaneously, using the commonplace materials she had at her disposal (markers, ballpoint pens, and drawing paper purchased in the stationery section of any drugstore), an exemplary body of art.

She didn't sign her pieces, asserting that her authorship was in the execution itself. It was natural, then, for us to consider creating an anonymous art whose presence would emerge as a *fait accompli*, no attribution possible, in the most public and culturally dead spaces in San Juan. The pieces, which would take countless patient hours to complete, were pasted up in a bus station or in office building restrooms; there they stayed as a riddle or a minimal revitalization of the space where we placed them. Why did we undertake this effort, which would bring us no benefits or be taken into account by those who wrote the history of these things? Suffice it to say that it was a form of love and of fury.

Our efforts grew in scale, and I became completely wrapped up in them. I dusted off my cameras and with Li's cooperation took close-ups of the cooks' faces in several Chinese restaurants. Some fifteen faces that rarely saw the sunlight, with pustules, spots, and bloodshot eyes, were replicated on hundreds of copies. Li and I spent early mornings pasting them up by concert posters and flyers for political rallies. No messages went with them. One morning this line of faces greeted the surprised gazes of pedestrians and drivers. On the radio some said they must be unknown candidates in the elections. Nobody, except for a couple of writers, imagined it might be a work of art. We loved the fact that, as the weeks went by, the images continued to be respected. Nobody ventured to draw mustaches on them or peel them off the walls.

On another occasion, Li sacrificed some thirty of her drawings of blotches, made with infinite patience, and pasted them on each of the doors to the apartments in a condominium on Avenida Baldorioty de Castro, which we entered by carrying the drawings and the paste hidden in a pizza box.

That was the only intervention at which Li allowed me to photograph her. In another half dozen images, you can see her organizing drawings, pasting them up, smiling beside an intervened door.

We also honored the way in which we had met when Li inscribed a series of phrases in her crude block letters, which leaned farther and farther as the line went on. Written in public places, on walls, on the sidewalk, the words became surreal. I remember several that must have revealed the skepticism of the citizens in different spots in the metropolitan area:

"Is a people that elects as its president an icon that has never read a book all that far away from burning books itself?"

"If there is not a single place where you have not suffered, what other motive can you invoke to justify living a life of wandering?"

I remember that Li particularly liked this one: "Men cannot clearly translate what it is I do, even if they are watching." That was the clearest possible definition of what we were trying to accomplish.

I have often wondered why we chose to remain anonymous. We probably expected near total incomprehension and indifference. Besides, I let myself get carried away by the wishes of Li, who found something voluptuous in disappearing. She'd used the same method in the messages she had sent me, and it had been in this way, by fading away, that she had managed to live her passions among the Chinese. Perhaps there was also, on her part, an intention of nearly absolute control. There was no greater personal authority than that of vanishing without a trace, as if none of the things that had been done with so much dedication and hard work ever existed.

The life of Li had been determined by events and commitments that bound her indefinitely. Immigration, poverty, family debts had meant a sort of servitude. What she was undertaking was voluntarily shrouded in mystery. She was putting together a play of mirrors in which, over the long run, there was no telling who was the person reflected, or even if there was anyone reflected. This way she could do whatever she wished, with no need for the understanding or approval of the rest. Her greatest efforts also required her to give up the most, but by doing so, she could be free.

One Saturday that Li had off and that we were going to spend together, I found a note when I went to the rooftop apartment to pick her up. She'd had to leave before our agreed-upon time to put in an order for materials for the restaurant, and she would be taking advantage of the trip to the Asian products store to visit with some relatives. She told me the hour when I should go get her at the distributor's store, which was across from the Isla Grande base.

It was the first message Li had written me in a long time. She had used ordinary, everyday handwriting, which made me miss the block lettering of the old notes.

It would be a while before I met her, so I took my time driving down Avenida Ponce de León to Miramar. I liked that route through town, especially when there wasn't any traffic. Coming up to the oldest part of Santurce, which had been built on a hill, I felt vibrations in the air and thought the light looked different than anywhere else in the city, probably because I was so near the ocean. Over the years, I had made this trip a great many times, especially on days I had free, to fend off boredom in a city that seemed dead. On this day, however, I had a purpose.

After parking, I went to a coffee shop to get breakfast. As I sat down next to the window, I realized that I'd been there a few months before, also on a Saturday, when I didn't know who the author of the messages might be. Things were fundamentally changed now. This realization made me smile, but it came with an uncomfortable premonition suggesting that all conditions and relationships are unstable. A few more months and I might be back in this same shop, listening to the incredibly childish voice of one of its waitresses yet quite far from the current order of things. This was a clichéd reflection, but behind its banality lay the brute fact that it was true. To that moment, I wasn't entirely clear what I meant to Li. We were living day by fleeting day, having made no plans for the future. We even did our art projects in the absolute present, no notes on the calendar required. I found this trend disquieting, as it embodied uncertainty. I had fallen in love with Li, I enjoyed every moment I spent in her company, and she didn't seem willing to discuss any sort of bond, not even one like a commitment to prolong our present situation. At times, I found this just as incomprehensible as the Chinese people she had lived with her whole life.

I walked to the Asian products store. I'd never been inside, but I had often seen the façade when driving down Avenida Fernández Juncos. On the same block there were a couple of topless bars and, a bit farther on, the empty lot where the city's largest brothel had once stood. At this hour in the morning, the area was deserted.

When I walked into the poorly lit place stuffed with merchandise, my first impression was that I had traveled to another continent. Tall display shelves, crammed with products I'd never seen before, limited the walking space to a narrow passageway. In the back, there was an old desk and a man who reminded me of Li's boss, but instead of his suits, this man was wearing a shirt covered in stains. Beyond where I could see, several people were having an animated discussion in Chinese.

I walked through the shelf-lined aisles, examining cans and bottles with labels inscribed in characters I found incomprehensible. I could identify their contents by the pictures but found it impossible to discern how they had been prepared. At the end of one of the aisles, I found a long, low table covered in newspapers and magazines, and above it a couple of small shelves with thin paperbacks. I took one. The cover showed some sort of mechanical superhero with a machine gun, and written on his metal breast in Latin characters, he bore the title of the adventure series: *Predator*. After the title page came the vertical paragraphs. Next to this tiny library were a good hundred videos, flanked by posters announcing martial art films from Hong Kong.

Farther back, past the boss's desk—I acknowledged him with a bow of my head—were more shelves where they kept dried fish, large bottles of sesame oil and soy sauce, woks and kitchen utensils of every size. I stopped for a moment to examine the rows of bottles that constituted a small pharmacy of Asian remedies. Behind a curtain an unknown number of children and adult seemed to be bustling about, and against the back wall of the store there was an enormous refrigerator, out of which emerged an older woman carrying bags full of vegetables.

Li was nowhere to be seen. I approached the boss to ask about her. He shouted something in Chinese; the woman who had come from the refrigerator answered him and then pointed to a door I hadn't noticed. Pushing it open, I found a staircase. The second floor led to a gallery around a tiny interior patio that marked the space between two buildings. Music or conversations could be heard coming from behind the doors. I knocked on one, which was answered by a man in a sleeveless T-shirt with a cigarette between his lips. Behind him was a narrow bed and a woman kneeling on the ground and facing a tub full of clothes and soap suds. The man made me repeat my question, then he went out onto the gallery and indicated with his hand that I should go to the end. I knocked on the last door, and when it opened, I found Li.

We did not kiss. Without a gesture from her, I knew that we were in a situation that called for extreme decorum. Near the small window, which opened onto the side wall of the neighboring building, were two men. Li led me to them. A short and very thin old man was sitting in an easy chair covered in clear plastic. On a chair facing backward rested a young man. The old man, named Wen Da, was Li's granduncle. Bai Bo was her cousin. I sat down on the rickety old bed. Li brought me a glass of tea before sitting down by my side. The relatives talked among themselves. Li seemed to be explaining to them who I was, but I guessed from the brevity of their exchange that this was old news and that their words constituted a sort of prologue. The two men must have been waiting for me.

Calligraphy, landscapes, and ink drawings of birds hung from the walls. Drafting implements were on the table, and in a corner by the door were about a hundred books organized into piles.

The old man spoke almost in a whisper, his voice hoarse. He was extraordinarily skinny, and his smile held only a couple of teeth. Through Li, he asked whether I liked the tea. Again, I raised the glass to my lips, tasted the harsh, earthy infusion, and nodded. Then he said that I would have health and long life if I drank several cups a day.

I noted that Bai, Li's cousin whom I had seen fleetingly around the restaurant, was glaring at me without ever directing a word my way. I played with my glass of tea, looked at the worn linoleum on the floor or out the window at the wall of the building next door, having no intention of getting involved in the conversation. After Li laughed with Wen, Bai said something that made her lower her gaze and answer with a short phrase that sounded harsh. Then he finished his tea and left without saying good-bye. From the doorway, he responded to his cousin. When he was gone we sat in silence.

—What happened? I asked.

—Forgive Bai, Li said after the sound of his sandals disappeared down the staircase. He's always been like that.

—It doesn't matter, I said, not understanding.

—Wen was an attorney in China, she said, changing the subject. But he also studied art. All the drawings are his.

I looked around the walls. The images were traditional: rivers, mountains, birds among bamboo shoots, examples of calligraphy that were probably the names of people or quotes from texts, all done with a skilled hand.

To say something, I asked him if he still worked at it.

—He says it is strenuous work, and he can't see well and is too tired.

—What do you read? I asked, pointing to the piles of books.

—Old books, Li translated.

We drank a second cup of tea in the old man's room. Wen Da was kind enough to show me his brushes, the rolls of rice paper, the inksticks. He searched through his books and handed me yellowing editions of Huanchu Daoren, Huang Po, and Chuang Tzu in the original language. Recognizing their names, I mentioned the Tao. Wen seemed happy that I knew something about the topic and spoke with enthusiasm. Li's translation was exceedingly laconic:

—He is talking about the Taoist practices he has followed.

—Why is he here? I asked.

—He came with our group, Li explained. He actually isn't my granduncle, but it makes no difference, I love him just as much. He worked in the restaurants with us, as a cook for many years, but he was different from the rest. As you see, he has books, and he's a painter.

—Do you come visit him often?

—Whenever I can. He's the only one I consider family.

—And Bai, your cousin?

—He doesn't count, like the rest.

—Why did he leave?

—He can't stand the sight of you.

—Seriously? It bothers him that you're with someone who isn't Chinese.

—It's more than that, and it isn't worth talking about. Bai, like all of us, has spent his whole life surround by woks or watching kung fu movies. He doesn't know anything else, and he's a pig.

—Did something happen?

—Lots of things happened, but it doesn't matter anymore, said Li.

The couple from the room next door was arguing in the corridor. Wen looked at Li with resignation. He took a five and several one-dollar bills from the nightstand and handed them to my girlfriend, who despite all her efforts could not give them back to him.

The old man told me to come back whenever I wished and to take good care of his "niece." We went downstairs to the store, Li held on to the invoice that the boss gave her, and, blinded by the midday sun, we went out into the street.

We spent the day wandering around old San Juan, eating sushi and ice cream in El Condado, visiting every bookstore we found along our way. There were few days when we had so many hours to spend together. Besides, I had the incentive of having met Wen Da and Bai Bo. Li had allowed me to come into contact with meaningful parts of her past, and I interpreted that gesture as a demonstration of closeness and commitment.

That night, we took a long drive, and I ended up, once more, asking her out to dinner. We were contented, Li had bought books and some clothes, and we had also confirmed that some of our graffiti pieces and interventions were still posing questions for the people who passed by. In the booth at the pizzeria, Li sat next to me, and I felt her body snuggling close, seeking my body's warmth. That night she would stay at my place, and she wouldn't have to be back at the restaurant until noon on Sunday.

The night was memorable. Something moved Li, who took more initiative than ever in bed. Her hands and legs, her whole body, pounded on me with a desire that set me aflame. It was a priceless gift. I lay face up while she slowly explored every inch of my skin, carefully gauging her movements to bring me again and again to the verge of blissful delight. She devoted herself to my pleasure, keeping my hands from working on her, as if she were determined to focus on my ecstasy that night. It wasn't enough for me to spill out profoundly and at length between her lips; she continued watching me without blinking, letting the sperm slip from her mouth to her breasts, letting me know by this that nothing separated us, that she was the only woman who could so enrich my flesh.

I woke from a reverie, a delicious prolongation of what I had just experienced, when I felt her once more between my legs, striving to revive my member, with a yearning that filled me and pervaded my body from head to toe. I didn't understand what she was doing, why she so wished for me to give myself to her, or why she insisted on possessing me.

I woke with no notion of how much time had passed, and I found her in my arms, asleep, curled into a ball, part of me. In the distance, the siren of an ambulance or police car wailed. Within me the terror that something might come between us was awakening. Lying still, listening to the nearly imperceptible rhythm of her breathing, I struggled to get rid of that fear, endeavoring to hold onto a little certainty. As I watched the nocturnal shadows of the trees dancing against the ceiling, I knew that my mind was trying to give birth to a thought that was taking forever to come. This was what had woken me from my sleep. I didn't know exactly what the thought was, and I realized at that moment that I didn't want to find out. It would be there, endlessly announcing its presence, in a mind poised at the edge of the precipice.

For weeks, we were deep currents traveling far in search of each other. We each possessed an elemental energy that flowed toward the other without seeking explanations. For once, during this brief period, neither past nor future counted for me.

I came to know the uprooted lives of the Chinese in Puerto Rico, the deeply introspective nature of their sadness, which they stifled in work days of ceaseless hustle. They were resigned to their lot and so exhausted that they had no strength left to desire any life but that of working in kitchens. This explained their endogamy, their slack efforts to learn a language or to go out and become acquainted, during their limited free time, with the society in which they had lived for years. In such a setting, Li stood out prominently, but it constrained her as much as it did them. She could only conceive of a different life if there were a clean break, if she left one day and moved as far as possible from the clan of which she had formed part.

I saw Wen Da a few more times, and I made friends with a group of taciturn and terrifying cooks who could be generous and loving when they thought about the wives and children they had left behind on a continent to which they would never return. Only Bai made no effort to approach me. He was a rough man, with acne scars and a premature bald spot, a few years older than Li. The other workers kept a bit of a distance from him. He was on the lowest rung of the kitchen hierarchy. After the restaurant closed, when they ate at the large table in the back, he sat in a corner concentrating on his bowl, almost indifferent to conversations. He hurriedly bolted down everything put in the bowl, as prisoners and some animals do. Whenever he could, he bet his day's wages on cards, played dominoes, or entertained himself watching martial arts movies. He spent his free day sleeping off the hangover from the night before. He and Li spoke rarely and with a curtness that was all too obvious. Only the boss's mother, who was his aunt, was well disposed toward him, to Li's displeasure.

We led a life that seemed much like any other couple's. My relative acceptance by the Chinese at the restaurant had made it possible for Li to spend almost every night at my place. I had to get used to going without much sleep, for it was after the night shift ended that Li arrived. We would eat and talk, and then I'd spend a while reading by her side. I would sense her toiling away at her ink and paper. Sometimes, deep in thought, she would silently move her lips as if she were speaking or humming. I would lift my eyes from my book when I heard her heave a long, deep sigh. She would then stretch her arms over her head, her breasts would stand out, and the cloth of her blouse would lift to reveal part of her belly and her hips. I would go to her, and we'd start to undress.

Other times, the scratching of the pen on paper was so violent that I knew the time wasn't right for amorous trances. I had to wait until her hands couldn't bear it anymore, which might take two or three hours. When she lay down the pen, she would be exhausted, but she would enjoy a peacefulness that she only experienced after her struggles with the ink.

The next morning, I would get up without waking her and get ready for work. By the bed, lying on the floor, would be the bag where she carried her clothes, books, and drawing materials. Li would get out of bed later and spend the morning reading. Later she would make something to eat and head off to the restaurant on foot.

We'd spend working days waiting impatiently for her days off. We'd get an entire day, and the morning of the following day, just for us. Our routine of walks, restaurants, and bookstores was set; we already knew we'd come back home to talk, read, and make love. The time we spent at night after dinner was a gift, hours that made us believe in redemption.

Encouraged, relieved by this normality, it was inevitable that one morning I would venture to bring up the subject. Afterward, I often regretted it, thinking my tactlessness had been unforgivable. Today, I know it was impossible, and therefore unfair, to demand that I act any other way. Since the night she had asked me not to penetrate her, I had sought an answer.

—You're never going to let me? I asked.

—Let you what?

In the tone of her voice, there was a sudden onset of panic, but by then, I couldn't stop. Just like me, Li must have been long expecting the moment when I would ask this question.

—Make love completely, I explained.

—I don't know.

—I love you, Li. It's natural to desire it, and for me, it's important.

—I guess so.

—So why not? We do everything else, and we enjoy it. I'm pretty sure you like it. Why not go that far?

—There are some things that are hard.

—Why don't you try to explain them? You shield yourself too much. You saw how close you got to me with the messages. You could have stopped the game at any point.

—But I didn't.

—I didn't, either. You hardly ever talk about yourself. I've learned who you are through what you do, almost never through what you say.

—I'm not accustomed to talking about myself. They say it's a Chinese thing.

—But now, you're with me, and it could be different.

—I know.

—It doesn't have to be today, think about it and trust me. What could happen?

—Everything.

We sat in silence. During the conversation, Li hadn't looked at me. Her hair hid her profile. I couldn't accept that she refused to clarify anything for me.

—Do you prefer women? Is that it?

—Sometimes I'd prefer a woman, but since I've gotten to know you, I'm not so sure.

—What is it that I don't know about you?

—Lots of things.

—What? I asked.

—What I can't tell you.

—And that is what? I asked bitterly, surprised by the emotion that overcame me.

—What I can't tell you, repeated Li.

The next day she let me know she was sick. When the telephone rang, after eleven thirty, neither the illness nor the distrust came as a surprise. She said we'd see each other the following night, when she'd be feeling better, but I was sure she wouldn't come then, either. Twenty-four hours later she didn't even answer my calls.

I thought it was unfair. What I had brought up wasn't a minor detail and couldn't be ignored indefinitely. I could even, at least I guessed I could, accept her ban, but she would have to show me why. What I couldn't take was a wall that constantly made me question myself. I had a pressing need to know why a woman who supposedly kept herself away from men had taken over my life.

Dark days followed when, as an ineffective antidote to her absence, I wandered the city aimlessly. At night, I would sit and write the story of how we met, as she had once made her drawings:

it was the tale of an obsessive line flowing out into an illegible geometry.

It was difficult to accept my failure in this way, with no explanation, no contact. I could no longer go through life assuming that nothing would happen, that my years in this city would be nothing but what I already knew so well that I was sick of it. Just wandering around streets and avenues with nowhere to go, in the vague hope I'd someday find a way out, a way to imagine for an instant she'd moved away and I might have another life or be in a situation that would really seem like another world.

The hope was vain and fruitless, but it was drilled into my mind and the minds of so many others, as if history hadn't allowed this society to come up with any other idea. This was one of the country's identifying signs; it was our obsession with salvation and escape.

I often remembered that I had to live in uncertainty. Li was shielding herself, but she would come back. It was hard to put up with at that moment, but I preferred the emptiness I now felt in my breast to the worthless time I'd led before meeting her. I waited. I suffered, knowing I had to keep waiting. I spent nights writing, expecting at any moment for the phone to ring and stop me, to tell me enough already. But Li never called, and I started to prefer her absence, the certainty that, once again, I had lost someone. Knowing that nothing would remain, that, for who knew how long, my life would once more go back to being a whisper, a blotch of slovenliness and forgetting, was strangely enough a sort of consolation.

I knew that Li was surfacing from the depths when on coming home one afternoon I found a black rectangle in my mailbox. She had pasted one of her drawings to it. It seemed to be from a new series, since the pen's fine line left many small blank spaces, and the impression that the blotch produced, a sort of cloud floating in space, had probably been created by writing and rewriting a phrase or a word. It was pretty good, and I was curious to see how this process would look in a larger format. On the back of the paper were the accustomed leaning block letters that hadn't been addressed to me since I had discovered the author of the messages. There were five short lines: "I have more opportunities to save myself through inferno than through paradise. Go to the Cine Paradise tonight and look for me at the image generator."

Li was returning to her old ways. I wondered, were we embarking on a more satisfying phase or regressing to the period before we lived together?

The Cine Paradise was in Río Piedras, and if my memory served, it was in ruins. As a teenager and young man, I had watched countless double features and a bit of theater there as the place turned over from one management to another, as its owners took a chance for a while on art movies and experimental film, or second-run Hollywood movies, or opted for the easy alternative of Italian films with steamy intimate scenes. In the end, the building that had housed so much fantasy had been abandoned to the incursions of bums and drug addicts until the owners or the municipal government walled up the entrances.

That night, I'd find out whether I was wrong and something new was at the Paradise. What was unmistakable was that this message lacked the magic of her old notes. Since I already knew who the sender was, it seemed unnecessarily roundabout. She could have phoned or dropped by my house—which was her house too, if she wished it—and saved me the effort of heading out and searching. Even so, I intended to go to Río Piedras that night, and my feeling of anticipation bordered on happiness.

I was ready early, but I delayed leaving because I wanted to straighten up the living room and bedroom a little. The days with no news of Li had produced their share of slovenliness. I dusted, swept, loaded a pile of laundry into the washing machine. I wandered through the house, waiting aimlessly for the dark of night to settle. It was after seven when I got into the car and drove to Río Piedras.

Avenida Muñoz Rivera was, once again, impassable. I had long since given up on understanding the logic of San Juan traffic. By this time, the bottlenecks caused by people leaving work should have cleared and the lanes should be flowing. I knew, however, that it took only one accident kilometers away or, inexplicably, an overcast sky, as was the case then, to bring traffic to a standstill. I crawled slowly past useless traffic signals, which, in the face of this onslaught of cars, had ceased to control their movements.

Turning onto Avenida Universidad, I found a similar situation. Río Piedras was awash with cars and pedestrians. People were milling about in front of bars, cafeterias, and grocery stores, overflowing the sidewalks, and I had no idea why there was so much activity. I took a side street and ran into another roadblock. I armed myself with patience, took lots of turns, and finally was able to park far away, on a street near the bus station, when it was already past eight.

I didn't know what was behind this influx of people into a part of the city that was normally uncrowded on a Thursday night. As I drew closer to the street with all the bookstores, which was also where the Cine Paradise was located, the throng grew thicker. I heard the sound of a woman's voice giving a speech and saw banners hanging from the streetlight poles announcing the first of a series of "Bookstore Nights." I understood why Li had called me there. She wanted us to meet in the crowd that would be heading to the celebration. It was one of the few times and places when books seemed to count in the city.

I came through Avenida Gándara to get to the stretch of Ponce de León where the bookstores are, for no apparent reason since it wasn't the shortest route I could take. This section of the thoroughfare, lying as it does within the urban core of Río Piedras, never struck me as belonging to the avenue that traverses the city all the way to old San Juan. This humble fragment where the main bookstores in Río Piedras stood really deserved to have its own name. It had so little to do with the rest of the avenue.

La Tertulia was crowded, both inside and out—lots of familiar faces I preferred not to stop and greet just then. There would be one or more book presentations there that night, with more of the same at Librería Mágica and perhaps other bookstores on the block too. The music was coming from farther ahead. There stood the Cine Paradise and the plaza by one of the Tren Urbano exits. The street was closed to traffic, and it was hard to walk along it due to the number of people. I was wondering how to get inside and meet Li through this crowd when I sensed I was being called. It was a young man who had read my books, a writer. Whenever I ran into him, he was nice enough to mention my writings. I talked with him for a few minutes before I could recall his name. Luis Rosario. He had a peculiar way of pronouncing the final syllables of words, his humble origins seeming to merge with a sort of pedantry. He was a tireless promoter of literary magazines whose few issues were published in towns in the interior and rarely reached bookstores in San Juan. He was taking advantage of our meeting to propose an interview with me that he would like to publish in one of them. It surprised me how large the meager reputations of writers from the capital loomed in the interior of the country. The opposite happened in the literary world of San Juan; here, you never lost an opportunity not to read or not to talk with a colleague. I exchanged e-mail addresses and telephone numbers with Luis and we said good-bye with a hug.

A few meters on, zigzagging through the crowd, I ran straight into a publisher who had no choice but to say hello. He had long stopped answering my calls, and the manuscript I had given him months earlier must have been lying in some corner of his office where he had paid it no attention whatsoever. He greeted me loudly, calling me "Poet," and embarked on a machine-gun fire of conversation, impossible to interrupt, in which he complained about losses in the business, announced new titles, greeted and introduced me to people walking around us, and finally said good-bye, insisting that I call him right away because we couldn't let so much time slip by this time without getting together.

I had to stop a few more times, for in the space of a hundred meters, there were countless colleagues from work, former students, people I had met over the years at exhibits, talks, and book presentations. On that night, the cultural world of San Juan, usually barely perceptible, was occupying the street.

Finally, I was able to reach the Cine Paradise. In the plaza by the Tren Urbano station, they had set up a platform and several food stands. A reggae band was playing a long, saccharine song, and everywhere you looked there were people eating snacks and drinking beer. The movie theater was just as I remembered it: a wall of unplastered cement bricks, partly painted over with a mural, completely blocked off the entrance. I stood there, listening to the music, standing on tiptoes to see whether I could make out if Li was anywhere to be seen.

Then, I sensed someone coming my way. Turning around, I found it was Máximo Noreña. Next to him were the children I'd seen him with a few months earlier at a shopping center and a woman who must be his wife. He asked me how he could get into the Cine Paradise.

—Is it possible to get in? I replied, not giving him an answer.

—It'll have to be possible, Noreña asserted, I have to screen a movie there tonight.

Having him there in front of me, I could see the mixture of ill humor and timidity in Noreña that characterizes so many writers. He had survived his demons and the lack of interest that long plagued his works, bound and determined to make books that recreated his most heartrending experiences. A fundamental malaise lurked in everything he wrote, but if anything validated his work, it was that he didn't run away from that pain; he was dedicated to nothing but exploring that colorless landscape, which he turned into literature. Finally, after years of work, he had achieved a relative success that had allowed him to imagine he was at least working for some sort of audience. He knew, however, that many readers and writers would have preferred it if Noreña had never come to formulate a literary universe in which the topics of the Tropics weren't enough to justify traveling there, unless you wanted to watch your pipe dreams fade away.

In recent years, he had made a few short films. Apparently one of them was going to be screened that night in the ruins of the theater that we didn't know how to get into.

—A friend also asked to meet me in there, I said. I was surprised because it's been closed for years.

—Well, tonight they're going to open it somewhere because they're thinking of restoring it, which is why they've organized this Bookstore Night. I'm Máximo Noreña. Nice to meet you. My wife, Isabel. My children. I've read a couple of your books. I recognized you from your book jacket photo.

—I've read almost all of yours. It's a pleasure.

—We have something in common, said Noreña. We've both at least made a gesture to these streets.

While we were talking, Isabel had asked how to get in.

—They say it's around back, she explained.

—Let's go together, if that's all right, Noreña suggested.

We went into the blind alley behind the theater. They had strung up colored lights in the back and people were milling around. The wind picked up and felt chilly for the season.

—I don't know the name of this street, I mean the one down there, said Noreña as we walked, but I remember that years ago, when I was still a teenager, there was a bookstore there. La Contemporánea, it was called. It wasn't very good, but the owner was a Spaniard who had lived in Cuba till the revolution. They called him "the Red." He had some sort of relationship with the woman who owned the Thekes because he used to be seen over there, too. Some of my friends were bold thieves. I'd go with them, but I never dared to steal one of his books. I always paid, and not because I had too much money. I felt that I had to protect the Red. I didn't want him to get upset, close the store, and leave us unarmed.

The anecdote throbbed with the tenor of Máximo Noreña's literary world. In it, bookstores, authors, and books lived side-by-side with the city streets and seemed to carry as much weight as characters and plot. Using other writers' texts, rereading them, altering them, he had created his own, in a society that had little fondness for books. He was a proud man and unquestionably had the arrogance of a person who had persisted in following his vision to the point of depletion and the pointlessness of a Pyrrhic victory. He had accepted, with a resignation that at times seemed like a display of ecstasy, the artist's marginality. In his books, San Juan was always the result of a writer's gaze. Somebody had once reproached him for that, to which Noreña had responded that others might found, build, and rule cities, but writers are the ones who invent them.

We entered through a side ramp and discovered a large space, like a small plaza. The theater seats had disappeared, leaving a large, empty expanse of cement flanked by tall, windowless walls.

—Look, there's no roof, said Isabel.

We looked up. All that was left were the steel beams, overgrown with creeping vines, through which the few stars in the cloudy sky could be seen.

—They should leave it the way it is, said the writer. Imagine this rude space as a stage to perform theater or dance, or simply to come and talk. A genuine ruin wouldn't be bad in a city that always turns its back on its past, that's happy to slap up a couple of condominiums and erase what had been. Any mayor would be capable of perpetrating a parking lot here.

More than a hundred people were strolling through the open space. Many of them were old enough to remember the hours they had spent there when the theater was still active. Máximo went up to the table where the organizers sat, the DVD of his film in his hand. His children were scampering around the open space and Isabel was saying hello to a couple. I walked through the theater looking for Li. I pulled the drawing out of my pocket and read it again: "Go to the Cine Paradise tonight and look for me at the image generator." I didn't have the slightest idea what the message might mean.

—Can you believe it? asked Noreña when he returned to where I was standing. They brought a projector but they forgot the sound system. They were planning to project my film as a silent movie. I refused, and they promised to find some speakers. We'll have to wait, but who knows how many people there'll be by the time they get them. Besides, it's going to rain.

—Let's hope not, I said, looking at the sky.

I walked around the place with Noreña. At the other end, where the lobby had been, we saw some stairs that had lost their handrail. It was dark. Máximo called his children over, and the four of us went upstairs, groping along the wall. At the top was the theater's small balcony, which gave us a magnificent view of the plaza formed by the nave. It was clear why Li had asked me to come precisely to this place: it was an unexpected, almost magical space to which I would have access only on this night.

Behind us, at each far end, were steps leading to two entrances without doors. Máximo asked his children to wait for him before going down, and he and I went into the room, which still had a roof and was completely dark except for the bit of light filtering through its tiny windows. We saw the silhouettes of two iron hulks. Noreña approached them and discovered that they were projectors, their machinery encased in rust. He was inspecting the enormous reels when I went over there.

—Impressive, he said. I didn't imagine they'd be so huge. To think, everything came through here: Italian neorealism, Fellini, Passolini, French New Wave, the soporific and vaguely pornographic comedies we killed so many evenings and nights watching. It's incredible they left this here.

—Yes, I said, watching him play with the wheels and handles, as if the projector were a salvageable monument and he were thinking about bringing it home with him.

—It was a great image generator. Dreams reached Río Piedras through here.

I was astonished. Máximo Noreña had just uttered the phrase that Li had written in her message.

—You said the same words that a friend of mine wrote this afternoon.

—Ah, really. Which?

—Calling it an image generator.

—It's logical enough. Almost an exact description.

—My friend asked me to come here, to the image generator, to meet her.

We were alone in the old projection booth. Outside, Noreña's children were bouncing something off the wall. Fewer people must have been walking around the theater because the noise had died down.

—There's nobody here, said Máximo.

—I know. It's after nine. Maybe I got here too late.

—She didn't say when? he asked.

—No.

—Well, your girlfriend's making things hard for you, if you didn't know the projectors were here.

—I didn't.

—You can't ask for miracles, Noreña concluded.

I hesitated to tell him the whole story. I thought that if anyone understood, it would be him. But I didn't say anything.

Máximo had gone out to see what his children were doing. I ran my hand over the mounds of rust on the image generator and looked around. The floor was covered with trash and piles of dry leaves. With my foot I nudged a piece of metal that must have come from one of the machines. I stood on tiptoe to look through one of the tiny windows. A singer was moving her hips in front of the microphone, accompanied by a guitar player with a mop of Rastafarian dreads. The crowd was dispersing, opening their umbrellas. The sky was pale with the reflected city lights. It was starting to rain.

I was about to go down to the balcony through the other door to the projection booth, when I noticed something lying on the floor and bent over to pick it up. It was a small sheet from a drawing notebook. At the top was a piece of tape. Li's block letters said, "La Tertulia. The third *Three-in-One*. Don't be late." The sheet had come unstuck, or someone had pulled it off.

When I emerged, Máximo Noreña had already gone downstairs with his children to the open space. I watched him talking with the organizers, who were rushing to pack up the projector before the rain became a downpour. The theater was emptying out, and the sound system hadn't arrived.

—The show has gone off without a hitch, Noreña said when he saw me. I guess we'll have to leave, he added, turning to Isabel.

—I have to meet my friend in La Tertulia. She left me a message.

—On the dream generator?

—I found it on the floor. It must have fallen.

—All right, then, see you later.

He shook my hand, and I said good-bye to his wife. As I walked out into the alleyway, I realized I hadn't asked for his phone number or suggested we meet again. I felt like a real imbecile.

When I reached the plaza where they had set up the stage, the drizzle turned almost without transition into a downpour. People ran for cover under balconies or in the train station lobby. The street, now empty of people, was a sea of trash and beer cups. The rain was cool, windy, laden with earthy smells. I couldn't wait until it died down, so I resigned myself to getting soaked. I arrived at La Tertulia with my shirt plastered to my skin.

Around the tables in the bookstore were more people hiding from the rain than book buyers, and Li wasn't in either of the two rooms. I took the message, which I had folded in four, out of my pants pocket and went to the Puerto Rican literature section. I looked through the shelves for the first letter of my last name. There was a small pile of *Three-in-One* copies there, placed so you could see the cover of the book. I picked up one and opened it, making its pages flip by quickly. Nothing in it. I turned back to the pile. There were five. The message mentioned the third one.

I picked it up and riffled the pages. I saw a vertical smudge that wasn't part of the book. I looked through it until I found the slip of paper. "You didn't come. Simone."

I had taken too long. It was the first time the Swiss clockworks of Li's messages hadn't worked, confirming that this was a time of missed connections.

The message found in the book was glacial. Its coldness was reaffirmed by the name she had used to sign it. It was as if the times had become confused, and it was no longer possible to tell which was really the present. One consequence stood out in this whole business: the elaborateness of her spider webs, in the context of our relationship at that time, bordered on stupidity. Li had vanished one day and weeks later had invited me to a place crowded with hundreds of people to leave me a message poorly taped in a hidden corner, which in turn sent me to another place. The process was pointlessly labyrinthine. Before, we hadn't met yet, and the messages created an exciting game of hide and seek. Now they were nothing but an unnecessary complication that could have been avoided by a phone call or a visit.

The tenor of the message gave no indication that she shared this reflection. Probably she imagined that I hadn't bothered to come, or that I'd arrived late on purpose.

I waited a few minutes for the rain to abate, leafing through the new books. When I saw that the cloudburst showed no sign of diminishing, I decided to go ahead and soak myself to the bone. The owner was standing by the door. Alfredo Torres knew everyone who bought a book, so after saying hello to him I asked if he had seen a Chinese woman in the store.

—Chinese? he asked, unsure what it was I wanted to know.

—Yes, Chinese, a young woman.

—Oh, you mean Carmencita's partner?

—Carmencita? I asked, not knowing who he was talking about.

—There was a Chinese woman here, Carmen Lindo's partner.

—Right, that's her, I replied, unsure whether it really was Li, jolted by this bit of information, which was news to me.

—She was around, Alfredo explained, but she must have left quite a while ago.

—You don't know where she went?

Alfredo shook his head.

—Hey, when does Carmen get back from California? he asked, but he didn't get my answer because I had run on.

The rain was intense. People were running around me under umbrellas or pieces of cardboard, laughing and shrieking when they stepped into puddles.

There was no point rushing since I was parked far away, so I soon slowed down and walked unhurriedly, almost content to feel the huge raindrops slamming into me, helping me not to think too much about what Li had decided I should not know.

I was practically alone in the flooded streets, and when I got to my car, I had to wade in soggy shoes through eight inches of water. The storm drains of Río Piedras were notoriously ineffective. After I sat down behind the wheel, I didn't take the shortest route down Avenida Gándara; instead, I drove around those streets, touring past the bus station, the Plaza del Mercado, the Plaza de la Convalecencia, just to see what the city looked like in the rain. I didn't want to go back home just yet. The night had been a letdown, except for meeting Máximo Noreña, to whom I had said a clumsy, rushed good-bye thanks to Li's complications. In the end, the only clear outcomes were our failure to meet up and the disturbing information I'd learned from Alfredo.

I drove past the Cine Paradise, since the police had opened the street up to traffic again. Near La Tertulia, I saw Máximo Noreña hugging the buildings to try to keep from getting completely soaked, with one of his boys in his arms and, behind him, Isabel and the older boy. I wasn't the only one for whom the night had turned out badly.

As I passed the gates of the university, I had an idea. Li had to have been returning on foot to the rooftop apartment above the restaurant, and she had likely been caught halfway home by the sudden downpour. She might still be walking back. I had to do all I could to find her. I needed to know why she hadn't told me about Carmen Lindo and what that meant. I remembered she had written in the message, "I have more opportunities to save myself through inferno than through paradise." I needed to know why.

I turned around as soon as I could and pointed the car toward Avenida Muñoz Rivera. I drove along it till I got to the sushi bar where she worked, but I didn't find her on the sidewalks or taking shelter in any of the bus stops. I retraced the route at top speed and then went along Ponce de León, which runs parallel. The wet sidewalks sparkled under the streetlamps, and there wasn't a soul to be seen. At the picnic tables outside the McDonald's near Calle Betances, I could see the silhouettes of some people sheltering under the meager roof. When I stopped in front, I saw, swathed in plastic bags, the fat, bearded vagrant who had been wandering the area for years, and a couple of men who usually begged for alms by the next traffic signal. I was about to give up my search when I noticed that, a bit farther down, half-hidden in a corner of the place, was Li. I braked abruptly and opened the door. She got in and sat down, completely soaked, trembling. I saw her eyes. She had been crying.

At home, Li took a hot shower and got into bed. A little later I lay down beside her. We both watched the shadows on the ceiling of trees dancing wildly in the wind from the storm. After some time, Li shifted positions and sought the warmth of my side. She fell asleep in an instant, without either of us saying anything about what had happened that night, without my having dared ask her if she had been or was the lover of Carmen Lindo.

Li's bag once more sat almost every day on the floor by the bed. Superficially, our lives went back to the way they had been before. We were each tied to our work and devoted our free time to each other. As might be expected, the recent events, together with our inability to clear up what they meant, created shades of gray and left us feeling somehow burned out. We weren't as fresh or as full of desire, and the silences began to weigh. Even so, I can't deny that I was happy to have her near.

Soon Li fell ill with a bad flu. Her aches and fevers made it impossible for her to work, and she spent days in bed. She would sit up to drink some broth or tea, we'd talk for a few minutes, and she would cover herself back up with the blankets. For endless hours, I could only see strands of her hair on the pillows. I started thinking she was pretending it was serious, or was willfully putting off her recovery, so as to have an alibi for a kind of domestic disappearance that would delay bringing up the subject.

For nearly a week, she didn't read or draw, and I was a shadow for her, coming in to ask her how she felt.

I took up her convalescence with an impossible combination of patience and restless anxiety. I wanted to imagine that life would give us a chance to start over. The days went by in a sort of dream state, and I convinced myself that waiting was the same thing as acting.

Between classes at the university, while driving, or when I woke up early in the morning for no apparent reason, I felt certain I was wrong. Deep down, I was frightened and acutely aware of our fragility. The small daily joys, the amorous trances, might last almost indefinitely, but there was room to doubt we had that elemental chemistry that truly unites two people. This question mark, which probably occurred to both of us, was a secret from which we irrationally wished to protect ourselves, as if the doubt were an affront and a betrayal.

We waited, simply waited, not knowing for what, not even having an inkling whether it would do us any good.

With the idea of freeing us from the gloomy atmosphere that had filled our spirits, on one of Li's free days, after she had recovered her health, I suggested to her that we should take a trip outside

San Juan. I was surprised when she agreed, given her scant interest in that sort of activity.

After taking her to buy a bathing suit, we took Route 3 toward Fajardo. I wanted us to spend a few hours on the beach and then eat in some village around there. On the way to the beach, Li seemed cheerful, her face bright. She continually changed the radio station and listened with the same pleasant attitude to a symphony, a silly love song, or a preacher's sermonizing. I was finally seeing her as she used to be.

I was worried that Li might get bored or feel self-conscious on the beach, but as soon as we got to the swimming area, I saw her exhibit the extreme pallor of her body with an unusual lack of inhibition. She lay down to catch the sun, splashed around in the shallow water, made sand castles, and went into the ocean with me until the water was over her head without getting alarmed.

At moments like these, she possessed an almost childlike charm. She was light and flexible, but at the same time she revealed a certain vulnerability, of which she probably was partly unaware, caused by her being out in the open. Her life had transpired in close quarters, restaurants, and rooftop bedrooms among a narrow group of isolated immigrants in a country that was very foreign to them. Though this contact with sea, sun, and sky—pivotal factors on an island—nourished her, she seemed to be missing her points of support and only momentarily inhabiting a place that would never be entirely hers.

Stretched out on the sand, I was watching her dig the moat for one of her complicated castles, and I realized how close I wanted to be to this body that simultaneously surrendered and withheld itself. I didn't say a word, but I fought insistently to find the form in which I could make my emotion evident. You know you love someone when you are afraid to make her suffer. There, by her side, blinded by the midday sun, I was anguished by a pain that was not my own, one that I could do almost nothing to stop. At this moment, Li was much more than a body I desired, or a Chinese person, or even a woman. Completely engrossed in her sand castles, she was then a human being whose secret pain I had glimpsed. Her circumstances, what she did or didn't do, what she knew or didn't know about herself, ceased to be relevant. She was plainly and categorically a living being with the ability to overwhelm me because I knew just how deeply she had been wounded. She was similar to me, without a doubt, but I desired more than anything, more than even my own happiness, that she not suffer, that she might be forever so: playing in the sand, as free from cares as the childhood that history had robbed her of. Love was, I realized on this beach, the impossible and failed attempt to protect someone from her own life story.

—You know something, Li? I asked, watching her through half-closed eyes.

—What?

—You're very beautiful.

She remained kneeling on the sand, biting a lip. I had never seen her blush before.

Later that afternoon, we went to one of the restaurants in Naguabo. We were ravenously hungry, and we waited impatiently for our snappers. I remembered I had last been there with Julia and Javier, more than six months earlier. After I discovered the author of the messages, I avoided them, and I finally had to explain the last time Julia called. Had I ever felt something like this about Julia's suffering? I guessed I had. The proof was this moment, when I was remembering her and wishing things had worked out differently. Had the women in my life shared this feeling? I couldn't be certain, but I suspected I hadn't always enjoyed that benefit, and this contaminated the memory. We live our love unconsciously, as pleasure, and what we miss upon its end is living bereft of memories, the life this small-format, manageable eternity created.

Li luxuriated in her meal, picking the fish's backbone, the salad plate, and the dish of *tostones* absolutely clean. Then she ordered a flan and nearly ordered a second. The sun had done her well, toasting her cheeks and shoulders, making her healthy and flush.

We returned to San Juan at dusk, when Route 3 was a pit of suburban melancholy. Li took the hand that rested on the gear shift and pressed her body close to mine. She was exactly repeating the gesture that had begun our relationship. I felt her very close to me, as if we were witnessing a new beginning.

After we bathed and settled in to spend the night at home, I noted something odd about Li. She was moving incessantly around the living room, rummaging through her bag, bringing a glass of milk and cookies from the kitchen, taking off clothes, changing clothes. She was choreographing a dance, and I was her only audience.

She finally settled on a pair of shorts and a sleeveless top, and she lay on the sofa in them. She stretched out her legs, waiting, lying in wait. This time she hadn't taken a book or the drawing implements from her bag, which she had left in the bedroom by the bed. I saw her smiling. I saw her make faces at me. I laughed when I saw her pantomimed boredom: fixing her eyes on the ceiling, she twiddled her thumbs, fingers interlaced, hands on her belly. With rare talent, accompanied in her case by a parody of common gestures, Li had a unique power of seduction. The messages she had used to kick-start our relationship weren't the only example of her abilities.

I fell upon her on the sofa and in a single movement we were joined, hands running under clothes that sloughed off our skin like paper wrappings. I took her breasts and sank my face, my chest, my groin in them. Our bodies moved like a sphere rolling from the sofa to the living room rug and then past it, onto the cold, naked floor. We didn't utter a word. We understood each other from our bellies, the muscles of our legs, from the insides of our mouths.

Holding tight, almost dragging ourselves, as if escaping a fire, we got into bed. Only our blind, fixed gazes through half-closed lids assured that this was not a fight, for we each moved the other's limbs with a force that, while striking no blows, respected nothing: no separation, no modesty, no limits.

Li sat down on me. I grabbed her hips, but she stopped me with a smack. My proud member slid over the sweat-drenched skin of her belly, from the top of her pubis to her navel. Then her arms immobilized mine. Her hair fell across and almost covered her reddened face, engrossed in what she was doing. Her lips were full and shone wet with her saliva. Alerted by the elation of pleasure, I realized we were on the edge of something unstoppable. Li was crossing a threshold and overflowing with an energy that would be impossible to subdue.

She took my member and brought it to her mouth. It was hers, it was something she massaged with her tongue, with its surface of wet and tenderly rough tissue; it was a piece of vibrant flesh for which she was the master builder. And then, in a movement that took one second but on which she staked her whole life, from the muddy rice fields on the outskirts of Beijing to the filth of the Chinese kitchens in San Juan, the rooftop bedrooms above the restaurants, the control asserted by her relatives and the loneliness, the pain, and the hope, she sat down once more on me, with one hand tight on the thing she would now not let go, using it to stroke the entrance to her sex.

So, with such absolute concentration that Li seemed lost beyond recuperation, breathing irregularly, about to weep, she let me, millimeter by millimeter, enter her, moving her hips just so, settling in, as if my member were a lost piece or the flavor of a fruit from another continent. When half was in, a single movement made me enter her and her body fell atop my chest. Then there was one second, an almost imperceptible pause, when we were both aware of what was happening and we knew there was nothing to be done. It was a magical moment, without a word, without a glance, without coming into the most absolute contact, a space that we were both discovering simultaneously and where we offered each other the freedom to lose ourselves in a pleasure that was almost self-absorbed. An instant later, back from the world we had glimpsed beyond time and identity, our hips were moving in a quickening rhythm that fought against pain and separation and became fused in our minds with ecstasy and perhaps also with love.

Her head was pressing against my neck, against my face, against my breastbone. Force drained from within through conduits swollen with pleasure in a wave of fury and jubilation that led to momentary spasmodic death in which life flowed out and, at the same time, was reborn.

And afterward, I learned that an indefinite time had passed when I felt her moving atop me once more, panting in a rhythm that sounded like weeping, while I rubbed her sweat-soaked back. "At last, at last," I repeated in my mind, as if that were the clearest statement of happiness. Then she lifted her head and found my lips and resumed the movement of her hips, rubbing my still-erect member against the semen-coated walls of her sex. And once more it was a body that was action and surrender, and I knew I was witnessing something whose forcefulness I would never be able to forget: this body, striving to breathe, bearing down on me and bathing me in its sweat, ready to burst, to come undone, to fall to pieces, with enormous hips that were focused on surrender and on sacrifice.

A noise must have awoken me. I opened my eyes and through the window I saw a patch of very dark sky indicating dawn was near. On the ceiling, the shadows of the trees were still on a morning without wind. Shifting my position, I discovered that Li wasn't there. I stood up, heavy with sleep. The light in the bathroom was off. Walking around the bed, I saw that her bag wasn't on the floor.

I left the room without a sound and walked down the hallway to the living room. There was a shadow in front of the door. In my mind, I immediately understood that something was breaking. I thought of all sorts of ways I could react, but opted for simply turning on the light. As if a lightning bolt had passed right over her head, Li wheeled around in fright.

—Where are you going? I asked. I stood naked by the dining table, before a woman who bore all her belongings on her shoulder.

—I was going to the restaurant.

—I don't think they're open yet.

—I mean, I was going to the rooftop room.

Li set her bag down and dropped onto the sofa.

—You think that's enough of a good-bye?

—No.

She shook her head with a whisper that contained the last word she was able to utter before bursting into tears.

I did not move closer. I let her choke on a wail that she tried to stifle with a faltering movement of her hands, which rose toward her face and did not reach it. I went to get dressed. On the way back, I stopped in the kitchen and poured two glasses of water. I put one in front of Li and sat on a chair. I knew the moment had arrived when all the questions would be asked, the ones I had avoided so many times and the ones I hadn't even seen coming until now.

I had no intention of consoling her. Her attempt to escape forestalled compassion. Nothing took its place. I felt a tremendous, almost inhuman pain, a hemorrhaging I had to ignore or else I'd fall apart.

For an instant, Li lowered the hands covering her face and looked at me. I waited a second before asking the question whose answer I hadn't stopped imagining.

—What did Bai do to you?

The muted voice came from a body doubled over, rocking back and forth.

—Raped me.

—When?

—When I was thirteen. Fourteen. Fifteen . . .

The words were cut short by her falling to pieces. She wept uncontrollably and seemed to be trying to hide in the very middle of the room as if my presence were hateful. But even so, she seemed willing to talk.

—So many times, rape probably isn't the word for it any more. We shared the same room, with other cousins. He would come to my bed when they were sleeping, and at first, I didn't know or didn't want to know what he was doing. Of course it didn't take me long to figure it out and realize it was something terrible, but how could I confess it, to whom. Not to my mother, who was still alive, I couldn't. Also, I filled myself with ideas, I was a silly teenager, and I guessed it must have something to do with love, with the things that happened and were always resolved in Hong Kong movies, when the characters didn't beat each other to death. It was also something to dream about, to forget the waste of a life I was living, waiting for him to climb into my bed. Bai was irresponsible and egotistic, but I had a secret bond with him, something that tied us together at night, when the rest were sleeping like the beasts of burden they were.

"They discovered us when I got pregnant, right after I turned fifteen. The boss's wife had them send her some roots from Hong Kong. She boiled them for hours to make a tea for me to drink on an empty stomach, ten days in a row. They locked me in a room on the rooftop, with nausea and pains, and I went half crazy. Finally the spasms came, and I got the worst fever I've ever had in my life. They took me to the Centro Médico right on time, because I was hemorrhaging. In the end the treatment was effective because I lost the baby."

I sat up to push the water closer to her. Li drank it and looked outside before going on.

—It marked me. You can imagine what petit bourgeois morality is like in such cases, but you have no idea what it, or rather the caricature of it, can be among a pack of ignorant Chinese. Bai was sent away for years to work in a restaurant in San Germán, in what you might call the end of the world. I didn't see him again until I was an adult. Fortunately, I did pretty well in school, and I found a refuge there, until I fussed and fought to get them to let me go to the university. But nobody was as close to me as before, and nobody thought of me as a victim. I was always surrounded by an aura of dirtiness and scandal. It was easier for them; they even got a kick out of it, and that way, they didn't have to come up with consciences of their own. My mother died feeling I had disgraced her, convinced I'd always be worthless.

"At the university I realized that something had changed, that many of my hopes and dreams were gone, and that now men were blocked off by a wall of terror and shame. I also found out, this is how serious my case was, that this was a possibility, that it happened to many other women, and that it was called lesbianism. I had a few flings with women at the university, but they didn't last long since in the end I was still the Chinese girl who worked six days a week and slept in a room on the rooftop. I must not have been much fun, and they really weren't for me, either.

"I hate the Chinese, it's terrible to say it, but it's the truth. I hate Bai and therefore all the Chinese who looked the other way as if none of this had anything to do with them. He destroyed a whole part of my life, a part I can never recuperate, that nobody, not even you, could give back to me. That's why I was leaving, in spite of what happened last night. That was my good-bye. I wanted you to know that I was ready to go where I never thought I could and also, though I'd rather not admit it, that I cherished some hope. I wondered what I would feel, whether Bai's body would interfere with yours, if I would get better or find the thing I don't know how to name and that I lost forever. I tried to talk to you about it so many times; I know you expected that of me, you offered me the opportunity, but the words wouldn't come. Today we did it, but it's as if my body had no reality. That body was there—I'm not nuts, believe me—it acts, it feels pleasure, but in the end it's a mirage. Something that isn't altogether there, or is like a tragedy for which no one is responsible.

"If anyone doesn't deserve my problems, it's you. It all started as a game, a very serious game, because your books bedazzled me, and when I learned who you were, I found you attractive. You don't know how I enjoyed fantasizing about a man again. I didn't think we were going to meet. Even when we did, I thought it wasn't happening. I was all alone then and didn't know what to do, and our getting together grew too quickly. Before, I had only fallen in love with women, and I was hoping that through you something different might happen. It's dumb, but a person has those dreams, those fantasies of being like everyone else again, as if it were possible or worth it.

"I don't know if I've used you. I don't know if the love I feel for you might be a way of using you. It probably is, and that's also why I was leaving. I admit it was a very bad way to do it. A while back, I was on the verge of a panic attack and at the same time completely numb. I'm not asking you to understand it or to forgive me. But I'm sorry I can't stay because if I stay, everything will be worse."

—And Carmencita? I asked, knowing she was only telling me part of the story.

—What?

—Carmen Lindo, the sociologist. Li and Lindo, sounds like a joke.

—She's met you.

—I know. We were at a conference. I didn't understand a word she said. Though she's a big fan of Derrida, or "Dérida," as she says.

—You shouldn't make fun.

—I thought you'd like other women.

—In any case, they wouldn't be the ones who appeal to you.

—Well, you have very bad taste.

—I don't care what you think. She was my professor, and she did a lot for me. Later we had a relationship. She went to teach in the United States. Now she's back.

—That's why you're leaving me. Because she came back.

—No.

—You mean, you're going to tell me it's a coincidence?

—Not that, either. Don't dismiss what I told you. I can accept your not understanding but not your taking me for an idiot or a liar. If your pride makes you see phantoms everywhere, that's your problem. Besides, this doesn't have anything to do with pride. I'm not who you wish I were. I told you from the very beginning: I'm lesbian. OK, a pretty liberal lesbian, and for that very reason a person with lots of problems. Carmencita and I have a history, just like you and I have one. I understand that you find this threatening and infuriating, but so does she, at least as much as you do. And now that you know my story, put yourself in my shoes.

—I haven't heard it all, and what I do know you told me very late.

—I did it when I could, and I don't think you would have preferred for me not to go to our first date in Castle Books. Besides, this isn't a matter of substituting one of you for the other. That's not it.

—So why were you running away after what happened last night, then?

—Precisely because it did happen, because it puts me in a situation that I don't know if I can be in.

—Why not?

—I already told you: because Bai raped me and I didn't protest, didn't raise the alarm, out of fear, out of shame; because I fell in love with a dog who only thought about what he had between his legs; because afterward I couldn't be with another man, and like any girl, I found them attractive, and I desired them; because I'm a woman who was never anything but the Chinese girl, in the neighborhood, the restaurant, the school, the comparative literature department; because I got close to women and fell in love with lots of them and they left me shattered; because of what's broken inside me and what I don't know if I'll ever be able to fix.

Dawn was breaking, and I went to the kitchen to make coffee. I watched the woman who had sent me the messages, and I realized I didn't know who she was. The woman I had imagined, the one who fit into my life, perhaps did not exist. The one who was talking before me now was a bundle of things I couldn't understand, who existed in a place beyond my reach, on the other side of a border that would probably always be there. This woman was a step away, sitting in the same place she had occupied on the sofa since I had discovered her about to leave, with her bag at her feet, and she was the absurd absence of a body I loved.

Some time later, I learned from the cooks that Li had gone up to the rooftop that same morning and knocked on Bai's door. As was often the case, he had gone to bed drunk on the eve of his day off. An intense argument had broken out, and the neighbors had been forced to intervene when Li began hitting him. The fracas ended when several hands pulled her away from her cousin. Then Li picked up her bag and ran off. She didn't show up at work that afternoon and only returned two days later, to her boss's great displeasure.

Afterward, nobody would tell me anything, even though I visited the restaurant several times over the following days. I gathered from the employees that Li wasn't there or was hiding because she didn't want to see me. I imagined that the foretold end was arriving in the cruelest way. As I drove around the city, I saw the now aged posters of the cooks' faces and couldn't imagine their having anything to do with me. I was turning into one more passerby, one more driver who didn't have the remotest idea what they represented.

I didn't even feel up to seeing Diego when he spent a few days in our country on vacation. The very idea of recounting the story of my relationship with Li—at the time, I wouldn't have been able to talk about anything else—filled me with a mixture of fatigue and feeling ridiculous. I had gotten carried away, such was the measure of my helplessness, by a charade of anonymous messages and had ended up getting burned by someone else's grotesque history. I made so many excuses each time we talked over the telephone that in the end I felt as ashamed as if I had told him every last detail of the affair.

For days at a time, my mind replayed the last hours I spent with Li. The morning on the beach, the meal in the port of Naguabo, the night, her body on mine, opening up all hopes. And then what had seemed incomprehensible and cruel, what had in reality been a desperate effort to give an explanation. I was wounded, stunned, victim to an unabating rage, but I also knew she had pieced that day together just at deliberately as she used to compose her messages. The day had been both a betrayal and a declaration of love. Realizing this was no consolation—nothing could appease me just then—but I recognized what she had done, her attempt to reach me by taking a step that would never be repeated. It was a gift. Something that shone in the midst of my squalor. But the trophy was horrendous.

Couples refuse to see it, but every love story has an ending. The unions that last an entire lifetime are survivors, stubborn fighters against collapse. And one of the rare glories of life is how they strive not to succumb. But the fact remained: love is a story, and stories always have their denouements. In the end there is death, physical or otherwise.

Like so many others, as long as I was in contact with the woman I loved, I remained stubbornly blind. It should have been obvious that we wouldn't be able to overcome our differences. Our sexual preferences were not some mere detail, nor was the emotional upheaval of living in the capital of our pain. This city, which overlay the city surrounding us, remained within us, occupying us with a hurt that was reborn with every new day. Besides, what did we want from each other? Had Li picked me because she imagined I could understand the tatters of her life? But indeed, could we share the same road? What did I know about her, when her courtship had been a disquisition on concealment?

I was tied to that woman, happy for the first time in years, but almost daily, before daylight broke or the alarm went off, a wave of anxiety would awaken me. I'd lie in bed, eyes open, without speaking, aware of the turbulent movements of my nerves, as if witnessing an undecipherable spectacle. In the twilit dawn of the happiest days of my life, I rehearsed the sinking feeling that had belonged to us since her first message.

I couldn't stay home, where the thought that I should be waiting around for Li tortured me. So I spent hours on foot and in the car, wandering the city, refusing any contact, my heart scabbed over. In this partial asphyxiation, I sought to dispense with other people, absenting myself from relationships, yet still inflicting my morbid disposition and baleful glares on everyone I met along the way. I knew that my actions were sterile, that the nastiness I aimed at the city's residents would meet with their indifference no matter how I insisted on scorning them. Nevertheless, I could not stop, and as I walked or drove, my mind reiterated the same ideas to the point of exhaustion. A motor thrown off balance by fury.

I ended up walking to such distant points that it took me hours to get back at night, sometimes in the rain and feeling wiped out. I went all the way to Carolina, to the center of Bayamón; as the sun set one afternoon, I found myself across the bay in the ferry terminal at Cataño. The San Juan metropolitan area was always a desert inhabited by imbeciles, and I knew that the worst of them all was me: that I was once again nothing but a mound of muscles and organs that, despite it all, continued obstinately carrying out their functions though I could provide them no meaning or repose.

One night, after roaming for hours, hungry, I parked the car in front of a Chinese restaurant on Avenida Esmeralda. There were other food places in the neighborhood, but I couldn't stand sitting alone at a table, reading the menu, and waiting for the guy to take my order.

Chinese restaurants provided the local version of fast, lonely food. The one on Avenida Esmeralda was like any other: Formica-top tables, false ceilings, neon signs, the small plastic altar behind the counter with a fake incense stick crowned by a tiny red bulb pretending to make a perpetual offering.

I ate with my eyes fixed on the paper plate, oblivious to the few people in the place at that already late hour of the night. As I dropped the fork onto the handful of rice I would not be eating, the memory surfaced. I had been here, in this very restaurant,

many years before, just before I started at the university, one summer night, with Diego and some other friends. Here, at one of these tables, enjoying some ice cream, we had talked about books and politics. I hadn't fallen in love yet, hadn't slept with a woman. Behind the counter, two teenagers appeared while we were talking. I observed the Asian girl closely, feeling the sort of sudden tenderness you only get when you've never known pain or disillusionment. Now, in the same restaurant on Avenida Esmeralda, I felt the insistent, imperious, anarchic certainty that the girl I saw then had been Li, that we had crossed paths for the first time many years ago as we each traveled along the force lines forming the city. The idea wasn't entirely harebrained. I knew she had regularly visited the restaurants controlled by her family clan when she was a teenager. The boy, deprived of features in my memory, could have been Bai. Perhaps I had seen them just before their catastrophe. Long after that time, I found myself here again, desiring the same body, filled with the same unanswered love.

Having no clear idea of what I meant to do, after I recalled or invented that first memory in the restaurant on Avenida Esmeralda, I began to retrace our steps. I returned to the Asian products store across from the Isla Grande base and asked the boss if I could see Wen Da. Seeing me by myself, he looked at me warily and told me to wait because the old man had stepped out. A few minutes later, the bell over the door rang and Wen walked in with a woman. Summer had begun and Li's "granduncle" was wearing a sleeveless T-shirt and a pair of shorts that looked more like old-fashioned underpants from which sprouted a pair of legs that were nothing but bones and thick veins. The old man didn't see me or didn't recognize me, for he stood right next to me in front of the boss's desk arguing about something. On his skeletal wrist, he wore an enormous old watch, its dial face stained entirely yellow. I'd never seen one like it, and I imagined it must be one of the few objects he still kept from China.

Finally, I decided to attract his attention, and I saw him focus his eyes, magnified by his glasses, on me. He immediately made a slight bow, shook my hand, and indicated that I should follow him. I picked up the bag of provisions that the boss had given him and followed him up the staircase to his room. That afternoon no one else seemed to be in any of the rooms opening onto the gallery.

We had no language in common. Wen knew no English or French and was barely familiar with a handful of words and expressions in Spanish, but I knew he might have me sit down and make me some tea all the same. I'd come to see him because of Li, but I had no idea whether this action would yield any results.

After we sipped the tea and I watched Wen rustle around the room looking for a roll of rice paper with his latest drawings, I became aware that we had never stopped talking. Each was interpreting what the other one said. Sometimes a phrase was complemented by a facial gesture or hands acted out a pantomime that might mean "I like that," "hot," or "many years ago in China." Wen spoke at length in his thin, hoarse voice, while his hands might form a school, a book, a town, a machine gun, a flood, or a deep sleep that might perhaps be death. When his hands imitated the rocking of waves and bodies holding tight to one another, I knew that he was telling the story of his journey to Puerto Rico. I recognized the long voyage, with stopovers, heat, and the overcrowding in the holds of the cargo ships, how he was treated by the police in an undecipherable country, a plane ride, and then the endless and indefinite kitchen work in restaurants, the same gestures repeated over a wok until your face becomes a mask of disgust. In response, I found myself talking, explaining who my parents had been, when and how they had died, and, with emotion constricting my throat, I said I hadn't gotten a chance to communicate to them my pardons and thanks, memories and longings, which their death had made pointless. When I finally stopped talking, the hand with the huge watch patted my hands. I lifted my head to see a man whispering words of comfort that I was, perhaps for the first time in my life, ready to receive.

We remained silent while he heated up more water. As he refilled the cups, he began to speak in a different tone. There was no mimicking now, no effort to overcome the language barrier, as if Wen had forgotten or no longer cared that I spoke no Chinese. Nevertheless, I knew what the topic was. In the words he spoke there was one that came up over and over and stood out clearly. It was his niece's name. I heard worry but also disappointment and sternness. I didn't know whether those judgments were also directed at me. I answered, I argued, I explained. Wen interrupted me when it was appropriate, when it was fitting to call me on something or register a doubt in the debate we were imagining. In the end, we sat in silence, looking each other in the eye.

Talking had done us both good. Something more real than languages, more elemental and powerful, had come about within these four walls of misery.

Then Wen stood up and pulled a portfolio full of drawings from under the bed.

—Li, he said, his only explanation.

I untied the cords binding the two cardboard sides of the portfolio warped by the humidity. There, in some disorder, were the drawings Li had done since childhood: typical school assignments, drawings of a flower or a house, mother's day or father's day presents, which in her case had been dedicated to Wen. Then the old man's influence became apparent, the niece's attempts to do landscapes of cliffs and mountains in the traditional Chinese style, and, after she had probably taken an art class, portraits of her mother, of cousins, and of restaurant coworkers, sketched in pencil on school notebook paper.

At the bottom of the pile were more recent drawings, done with better materials. Among them were her first attempts at abstraction: labyrinths of lines, compositions with solid shapes painted in tempera or watercolor, aggressive machines inspired by surrealism.

Separated from the rest by the wax paper in which they were

wrapped were some twenty pieces, done recently, because I recognized the paper and knew we had bought it on one of our outings. They were a variation on the usual dense blotches, seemingly made with the same stubbornly insistent line, but in this case leaving more blank spaces. At first sight, they looked like netting or honeycombs, but on closer inspection I realized they were formed by superimposing written phrases. Something was there in them: a word, a sentence, or an entire paragraph that had been written systematically over and over again until it became unintelligible.

The last dozen drawings were nearly identical, and it was logical to assume they constituted a series. They were denser and blacker, as if Li had tried to solidify the words. I inspected them with growing interest, suspecting that there was a message in them that Li had determined would not be read. One corner where the lines of the word had been written and rewritten less intensively gave me the clue. There, unquestionably, was the form of a *b* and the dot of an *i*. I checked and saw the pattern repeated in other drawings, perhaps five or six of them. This was how I found out what Li had been secretly drawing all the months she'd lived with me. She had written Bai's name countless times, trying to erase it, cross it out, crush it into a solid blotch. The result was a rectangle of black lines that looked like a tombstone, her attempt to destroy the past.

At the very bottom, there were three or four more pieces that, while made in the same way, expressed a different dynamic. It wasn't easy to decipher them, either. The word that formed them was finally made clear by the curve of the *c* and the straight lines of the *m*. Li had written Carmen until she had cancelled out the name. It had been her attempt to prevent Carmen from returning, to ward off what she feared would happen. This was how she had meant to save us. These sheets of drawing paper, bought by the two of us, bore living witness to her silences.

When I closed the portfolio, I saw that Wen was watching me. He uttered phrases, laying his fragile hand on my shoulder. I kept nodding as if I understood and agreed, now that I understood that I wasn't a victim of abandonment but of a war that had been lost.

After my visit to Wen, not only did the same questions remain unresolved, but I felt an even more urgent need to find some answers. It wasn't enough to have seen Li's torment expressed in her drawings. The fact that a woman shattered by men had decided, with much premeditation, to have a relationship with me remained a deep mystery. Why had I been chosen? Invoking random chance or accusing her of thoughtlessness resolved nothing. None of those explanations clarified our history together. Besides, why had she allowed me to penetrate her with devotion, passion, and delight, when Carmen Lindo was about to return and Li had decided to go back to her? Why was she sacrificing me? Why was she, as I was convinced, sacrificing herself? I had already glimpsed an explanation when I visited Wen at the Asian products store. Now I needed to know more, whether or not it would do me any good.

During the first days after she disappeared, when I went to the restaurant to look for Li, I had run into the imperturbable faces of the stressed-out boss and his wife, who shed no light on the subject and tried to keep me from talking with the employees. It was unlikely in any case that the cooks, who had been pretty friendly with me, would be able to clarify things, given how limited their Spanish was. But I didn't even get a chance to find out. Then I remembered the Dominican woman who took orders on the side of the double restaurant with the cheap menu. She was a friend of Li and must know something.

Just an hour before they closed, I found myself in front of the shuttered entrance to a building across Avenida Muñoz Rivera. The windows on the expensive side of the restaurant, where Li had worked, were darkened and nothing inside could be seen, but the neon lights and plate-glass windows turned the other part of the restaurant into a sort of light box. Three lone diners and one couple sat in the booths. The Dominican woman sat reading behind the cash register. In front of me, at the traffic light, an addict mechanically begged, using a paper cup from the restaurant.

While I waited for closing time before crossing the street and walking in, I remembered how often I had ordered food from the Dominican woman, never imagining that someday I might be begging her to answer my questions. Li had mentioned her once or twice. Her name was Glenda and she studied at a beauty academy. She was my last resort.

Shortly before ten, when only one diner remained at a booth, I entered the restaurant. Resigned to waiting on one more customer just before closing, the Dominican looked up from her book. When she saw who it was, she stood.

—Li isn't here, she said before I had a chance to ask anything.

—That's not why I'm here. I'd like to talk with you, if I can. You're Glenda, aren't you? Li told me about you. I know you're friends. I'd like to find out about a few things. That's all. It'll only take a minute.

—That's OK, but not here. They fired Li and the boss won't like seeing you in his restaurant. Wait for me in front of the fire station. I'll be there in ten minutes.

It was late and the stores around there were closed. Since I hadn't brought the car, I suggested to Glenda that we go to a park in the neighborhood. It was one of those spaces hardly anyone used now that people were accustomed to living indoors. At its center stood a gilded bust with a congested head, huge and horrendous, covered in pigeon shit. It was Rubén Darío.

We sat by the basketball court under the light of a lamp post.

—You must know, I have, or had, a relationship with Li? I asked.

Glenda's smile convinced me that she didn't mind talking with me. She was maybe a couple of years older than her friend and was very unlike her. She dressed very flashily, her long nails painted with a wing design and her straightened hair dyed red. It was clear that her dream was to work in a beauty salon.

—I've known all about it since before you guys started, she said.

—What do you mean?

—I mean Li told me all about you two. We're friends.

—But what do you mean, before we started? I asked.

—How she met you, the little notes she left for you, how she'd hide to watch you . . .

—Tell me. Li hardly told me anything.

—That *chinita*'s crazy. She gobbled up a book by you, a real, real sad one, and went around mooning over your photo. Since she was going to the university then, she saw you over there and saw how you spent all your time walking around. Around Ponce de León, around Río Piedras, around Santurce. She got curious why you did it, why you wandered around with nowhere to go, always by yourself. Since she'd shown me your photo, I realized you came in sometimes for a fried rice from the restaurant, and I promised Li I'd let her know if I saw you. Sure enough, one night you came in and I ran out to tell her, but then the boss complained I'd left the customers waiting. Li came over and stood there eyeing you from the door between the two places.

"We spent a lot of break time imagining who you were and why you were alone. I guess you know Li doesn't like men, well, before she was with you, she said she didn't like them. That's why when she told me she was writing stuff for you and leaving it where you could find it, I thought she'd gone crazy or she was in love. Everybody's time comes. Even for women who don't know they're ambidextrous, apparently.

"I kept up to date about the hunt the whole time it was going on, and I went with Li more than once when she hid out and spied on you to watch your reaction when you opened the envelope or saw what she wrote on the ground. My being there was also good to throw you off the trail in case you saw us at it, since it meant Li wouldn't be alone, and you couldn't tell which of us was the one with the messages. But you never caught on to us—you're so dumb—and we had lots of fun. Sometimes I told her: Li, stop bugging the poor guy, go introduce yourself to him already. What could go wrong? He's weird, but so are you, and you like him.

"But Li kept on reading and rereading whole books, and writing little notes that she'd leave for you God knows where. And so on, till you guys met in San Patricio Plaza. My cousin loaned me his car so I could drive her there and back that night. When she told me she had left without saying good-bye, I gave her a good talking to—after disappearing like that, I thought you'd never give her the time of day. But that didn't happen, you were too patient for that, and, well, you know the rest of the story."

—Not the whole story, I said.

—If you want to know more, if that's why you came to see me, I can tell you Li loves you, and she was happy with you.

—So why did she vanish?

—Because Carmen came back. I don't know if you know who she is. She's the woman Li was with before you.

—You think it's that simple. Li goes back to her old habits and just like that forgets what happened between us.

—Yes and no. You're strange; Li's even stranger.

—Why go to Carmen now? Hadn't they split up?

—They've known each other for years, from back when Li started college. Carmen influenced her a lot, apart from helping her in more than one sense. Among other things, she ended up paying Li's tuition. You should know that Li doesn't have a penny to her name, and the Chinese, especially the guy that owns the restaurant, are slave drivers. Me, they pay minimum wage, but the Chinese don't even get that much.

—What you're telling me is, Li is extremely grateful, and she has debts.

—Right, both those things, and of course more than that. It's not so easy, like you say.

—Why did she leave, then?

—You want me to tell you the truth? asked Glenda.

—That's why I came.

—Because she was scared.

—Scared of me?

—I don't know, maybe that too. But mainly scared of the Chinese.

—I don't understand.

—Li doesn't have anybody, Glenda explained, and the Chinese are her world.

—But you said they fired her.

—Yeah, but that was just the other day. There were problems, and the boss's wife never liked her much. She couldn't understand why she wanted to study and be different. Besides, after she left your house, she missed work, and that's something the bastards never forgive. They're mules, and they think the rest of us should work like them.

—Well, there's no reason now for her to be as scared as you say.

—Just the opposite. Now's when she'll be running to the bathroom.

—Why?

—I already told you. Because she's alone, she's got no home, no money.

—Where is she?

—With the professor, Carmen Lindo.

—Why with her and not me?

—That I don't know. You'd have to ask her yourself.

—But why do you think, given all you know?

Glenda thought it over for a while, straightening her necklaces, playing with the pages of the book she had set on the bench.

—I think, let's see how I can put it for you, she wanted to escape.

Something flew over our heads and settled in the trees. Glenda grew anxious and wanted to leave.

—Don't worry. It was a bird, I said, trying to calm her.

—No, they're bats. They're going to get tangled in my hair. I should be leaving now.

—Where do you live?

—On Roosevelt. I share a room with a friend.

—I'll walk you if you'd like.

We went up a street that was a long, perfectly straight line. I thought it was the most unnatural thing that could exist. Maybe that was also why the city seemed so disagreeable. It was constructed along a model that didn't correspond to life.

—Have you been here long? I asked while we walked.

—Six years since I came on a yawl.

—Have you ever been back?

—I can't. I couldn't ever go there and sail back here on a yawl again, no way.

—Do you at least have some family in Puerto Rico?

—Aunts and uncles, but I left my little boy in Santo Domingo. Look, here he is.

Glenda took out a photo. Her son was posing in the very center of a vacant lot. The image appalled me.

—What's his name? I asked.

—Jean Michael.

Glenda put the photo away and added,

—This is no sort of life.

—I guess you understand the Chinese, then, I said.

—Of course I do, even if they're assholes. They got it worse than us because they come from the other side of the world, and there's no way of getting back there. God willing I'll get to go to Santo Domingo next year and come back here with my boy. Them, forget about it. What I say is, we don't work so much for ourselves as we work for Western Union.

—Do you think I could see Li again? I'd like to talk to her. I don't mean to screw up her life.

Glenda thought about it for a moment.

—I didn't tell you this, but this Saturday night, there's a party at Carmen Lindo's place. That's 31 Calle Canals, third floor. I'll be there, but you never met me. OK? Don't even think of saying hi to me. If I was you, I'd show up and introduce myself, they aren't going to kick you out.

We stopped in front of a garage door.

—Here it is. The little place in back, she explained.

—What are you reading? I asked.

Glenda displayed the front of the book.

—I borrowed it from one of the cooks. It's good.

The wrinkled, dog-eared cover showed a landscape of skyscrapers in flames and, in large letters, the title: *Predator*.

Saturday afternoon came around, and I still hadn't decided whether to go to the party. I wasn't in the habit of showing up unexpectedly at places where I hadn't been invited. I spent hours doing nothing but struggle with the question. I was afraid of causing a scene that would give Li an excuse for leaving me once and for all. Most of all, the thought of letting outsiders see the pain I was living through genuinely horrified me. As the sun set, I tried to convince myself, telling myself Li had spent weeks hunting me and I could let myself use a similar strategy with her. I tried to believe I'd find the courage to enter the elevator and knock on the door. In my anxious state, that was the biggest stumbling block, and I didn't know whether I would be able to overcome it.

I stalled for time by driving around the block. At around eight, I parked and walked to Calle Canals. Number 31 was a five-story building with a rooftop terrace shaded by panels of corrugated iron. At street level, there was a dry cleaner's and a small supermarket, still open at this hour. My head felt light and my heart was pounding.

On the third floor balcony, two doors stood open. Reddish light and a hint of Arabic music filtered out through them. Shadows moved across the bit of ceiling that could be seen in the apartment. The shadows were far apart, so I supposed that most guests hadn't arrived yet.

I noticed three people coming in my direction on the opposite sidewalk. I took a few steps back and hid among the bags of garbage from a clinical laboratory. When the man and the two women drew near, I recognized them as professors at the university. The bald, chubby man with very white skin was an economist, and he could have once been called an acquaintance. More than ten years had passed since we last talked, however. One of the women must have been his wife; the other was a psychologist who had vanished into administrative positions and who liked doing academic tourism to assert, in select cities, that a better world was possible. This must, unfortunately, be Carmen Lindo's social circle. The established and slothful professoriate, with short and dubious lists of published works, prone to attacks of gout, intellectual paranoia, and menopausal hot flashes.

From my hiding place, I saw others arriving who were cut from the same cloth. Not all of them lived and worked in the country. The arrival of summer allowed people to attend the party who hadn't found work in the country and had emigrated to institutions in the United States. The incestuous and complicitous atmosphere they would bring to the party was completely inappropriate for my meeting with Li.

I left my hideout ready to turn around and go home in defeat. That was when I saw a man walking from Avenida Ponce de León. When he was twenty steps away, face lit by the street lamp, I recognized him as Máximo Noreña. He must have seen me from farther back because, without shifting his posture or raising his eyes, he walked straight over and welcomed me.

—Good evening, professor, he said, shaking my hand.

—What are you doing here? I asked.

—You also look like you were forced to go to Carmencita's thing.

—In a way, yes, I replied, not wishing to go into details.

—It could be dreadful, you know. It seems that the appearance of a visiting writer from Spain is the sort of event for which one must drop everything and come running. Carmen called me at home at least twenty times to make sure I'd be here. I guess she is supposed to provide the novelist with indigenous literary specimens. At least we know his name, and some of us have read his books, but he won't have a fucking clue who any of us are. There's nothing like that difference to foster literary understanding, especially since he'll interpret his ignorance as proof of his superiority. If he hasn't read us, he'll think it must be for good reason. These situations put me in an exquisitely bad mood and I'm afraid the night will turn into Madrid versus the West Indies, a reprise of the Conquest, with a possibility, I hope, of rewriting history.

—Who's coming? I asked.

—Don't you know? Noreña was surprised. A real somebody: Juan Rafael García Pardo. I thought they must have reeled you in, too.

—The one who wrote *Time for Good-bye*.

—Yes, and *You'll Never Go North Again* and other annual offerings, all equally irredeemable.

—He's not very good.

—He's Spanish.

—What more could you expect, I said, laughing.

—Naturally, but don't tell him so, because he's on an evangelical tour paid for by his country's Ministry of Culture, and he might take us for envious pygmies. I'm sure the first time he gave a thought to Puerto Rico was when he got his ticket on Iberia.

—Probably.

—You want to grab something to drink? Noreña suggested. We'll have to go upstairs after, and it's better not to rush it.

—Of course. Where should we go?

—There's a cafetería on Ponce de León.

When we sat at a table near the bar in the outdoor café, I felt good to be away from that building. Máximo got us a couple of beers.

—For many years, I thought what I missed the most about Europe were the cafés, he said. But when I had a chance to go back there, after a ton of years, I found that even those no longer held up to my memories of them. Now I don't miss anything—not because this is any better but because just about everything has the same feeling about it and makes you feel like you haven't traveled anywhere. Europe, the Europe you have in your head, which is basically an invention of literature, may have once existed, but I'm definitely not interested in looking for it or in finding it, either.

—You're exaggerating a little, I said.

—Of course; exaggeration is a literary genre, Noreña clarified.

What I'm getting at is that over there they have no idea how close they are to becoming imitations of us. We're used to being worthless and to the poverty of earthly joys, but they aren't. Here we know, at least anyone with a bit of perspective does, how rare it is to find a situation favorable to life, creativity, or what have you. If you are a writer, this is painfully obvious. But they're blind. They still put their faith in the prestige of their traditions and in the symbolic (and to be perfectly clear, little more than symbolic) position their societies grant them, even if that is more out of inertia or custom than for any other reason. García Pardo, who lives from his writing, though not from his books but from the brief articles he publishes in the press, will refuse to see himself in this light and will think that he's several steps above our situation. We aren't subsidized by anybody, and we can't write for a press that is pure garbage, and our books hardly exist for anyone. We're a geographic, political, and literary island. But there isn't a huge difference between the situation of a writer from Spain or whatever and us, though they'll never be able to see it. And I'm telling you the truth: I prefer the clarity of being on the margins, in this squalor.

—They're professionalized over there. In countries like Puerto Rico, it's very hard to attain anything like that.

—That's true, but it's a precarious professionalization, filled with concessions and renunciations that make it nearly pointless. That's the problem, right there. García Pardo can't complain because he runs to pick up the crumbs they drop for him from the table. He isn't free. He isn't a writer so much as a hack who makes a living from filling a given number of column inches in the papers with sentences, and that is precisely what they look for in the people they contract, to fill paper with the dead letter of common wisdom.

—It's preferable to what we've got.

Máximo Noreña looked at me as if he were examining my intentions, fearing I didn't understand him.

—Let's be clear about this, he said. We're a half-formed

country—that is, a society that's never been able to think of itself as anything but a province. Our institutions, when they exist, fit that trend line. They can't see past it. When the statehooders are in control, they don't even go that far, and we get four years of self-destruction. If instead of being Puerto Ricans, we were Galicians, Serbians, Nigerians, or Costa Ricans, there wouldn't be any huge differences. They also get the small publishers, the small reading publics, the nationalism for idiots, the isolation, the myopic administrations. The thing is—let's take the Spanish case—is that they have centers, Madrid and Barcelona, with real cultural industries. Those are the major leagues, the Division I, and everything within them conspires to make you think you're writing for the whole world.

—That's one way to understand the disappointment their literature produces, I said.

—But have you read Juan Rafael García Pardo, whose name is too long for his book covers? It could be him or plenty of others, doesn't matter. He has a culture, let's call it "world culture," that has allowed him to produce a presentable, even fairly decent text. But I insist, it's that "world culture," the fruit of a more or less effective school system, that allows him to dream of a Europeanness that is more a brand image than a sign of genuine prestige. I suppose he can identify the parts of a Corinthian column or a Romanesque cathedral; he'll play up the legacy of Cervantes and the Golden Age, then jump ahead a few centuries to the Generations of '98 and '27, and he's convinced that this tradition lends more authority to him than to others. Apart from that, he probably has a schoolboy's French, old summer trips included, an adolescent fascination with New York and US cinema, and at opportune moments for bulls and flamenco. So he can write about fine wine or about terrorist attacks, whichever, and he constructs *his* Civil War or *his* version of the North American novel, in that hereditary language that sounds like it was snatched from a lawyer's office.

Máximo Noreña's arguments were leading him to a dead end. I saw him struggling against something enormous over which he had no control or influence. Nevertheless, behind the harshness was the passion of a man who was staking his life on a text.

The writer had set a clear plastic bag of small cigars on the table.

—Mind if I have one? I asked, carried away by an impulse produced by the tenor of that night.

—Please do.

—I'll light it in a minute, I said when he held out the lighter. It's been a while since I've smoked.

—I've gone back to it, he explained. I return to tobacco as passionately as I give it up. It's a writer's vice, and I don't think I'm just repeating clichés. Smoking produces a low-level anxiety that helps prevent me from leaving my desk and keeps me facing the paper. To write is to wait, to stick around until something turns up. You have to be able to master the dead time between paragraphs or even between words. Smoking helps you to put up with the waiting, stare it down, be stronger than the silence.

—When you stop smoking, your writing changes.

—That's what I think. At least you stop writing with the need to find something, somehow or other, no matter how long it takes, regardless of how your day is going. When you smoke, all days are alike and so you can limit your activities: smoking and writing. Everything else is extra or doesn't count. So you go on till you can't take it anymore, till the tobacco is as worthless as continuing to write. I quit when I'm too worn out, so I can go back to smoking and writing later on, as if I were always returning to the moment when I started doing both things, so many years ago.

—How do you know Carmen Lindo? asked Noreña when they brought us the second round of beers.

—I don't know her, I answered. I went to a conference, and she was there. That's all.

—Weren't you going to her party?

—I was planning to show up there uninvited because there's a woman I have to talk to.

—I might have guessed, since the university bigwig scene doesn't suit you any more than it does me. Who's the girl?

—Her name is Li Chao.

—She was my student. Extraordinary, that Chinese girl.

—I know; that's why I want to see her.

—Is she your partner?

—Is, was, I'm not sure. That's why I want to go up there.

—It's none of my business, but did you know she's Carmen's girlfriend?

—Yes, but she was with me until a few days ago, and now, I'm all messed up.

—Happens to all of us, said Noreña. Let me warn you, professor Lindo is going around telling everybody, with the falsest modesty I've ever heard, that she's been given a contract somewhere or other and she's moving "once and for all" to the United States.

—First I've heard.

—You have a few things to clear up with your girlfriend.

I lit the cigar and, as I inhaled the smoke, the walls of my mouth awakened from a long sleep.

—We'll tell them you're with me, said Noreña. I'll introduce you to Carmen myself.

Polishing off his beer, the writer spoke again:

—Know why I have to go to the party?

—You said they called you.

—That's right, but it isn't the reason.

—What, then? I asked.

—I can't say no to Carmen. A long time ago, when we were students, Carmen and I had a relationship and came close to getting married. Books brought us together and women drove us apart. You aren't the first or the only one.

When Noreña and I got back to the building, I saw lots of shadows running across the apartment ceiling. Two couples were waiting for the elevator in the lobby. One of the men was the rector of the university; the other was a lawyer who had a political commentary program on the radio. Noreña took me by the arm and led me to the stairs.

—Let's go up here, he said. I don't want them to pretend they've read me.

From the second floor landing, we could hear music and the sound of conversations. The apartment door was ajar; the people who had been waiting for the elevator must have just gone in. Noreña held the door to keep them from closing it and entered first.

—Hello, how are you? he said to someone I couldn't see. I want to introduce you to a friend.

The writer nudged me on the shoulder, and I found myself face to face with Li. Noreña told her my name, also adding that I was the author of *Three-in-One*.

—I think I told you about him once, I'm sure you'll want to talk with him.

—Nice to meet you, said Li, shaking my hand and pretending to meet me. When she brought her cheek close for a kiss, she whispered in my ear, What are you doing here?

—I came to see you.

—You think this is a proper time and place.

—You've given me no other option.

—You should leave, you might create a problem.

—And you haven't created one for me?

Noreña had left us, and we could hear him greeting Carmen in the living room.

—Come, he was saying, I want you to meet a good friend.

Noreña returned to the foyer, bringing Carmen along by the hand. She was looking back as she came, as if to judge the success of her party from that perspective. When she heard my name, she spun around, and I found myself before a woman confronting an emergency.

—I wanted to bring him with me, Noreña explained. I hope you don't mind.

—Of course not, Carmen lied. Hello, welcome, she added,

greeting me. Li has told me about you. I wanted to meet you, and besides, it's important for you two to talk. I really don't mind. Just make yourself at home. Right, Li?

Li nodded. An awkward discomfort settled on us all.

—I'll leave you two. I have to go see the rector, said Carmen, adding to Noreña, García Pardo is already here. Come meet him when you can.

—And so? I asked after we moved to the relative privacy of the hallway.

—And you? Li retorted.

—Bad.

—I'm sorry. But you shouldn't have come.

—It seems you don't like trading places.

—This is not the same thing.

—Oh, isn't it?

—Because we aren't alone.

—It would have been nice of you to have told me.

—I couldn't.

—And I pay for the broken dishes.

—And me? Nothing.

—You ought to know.

—You're being sweet.

—You, clever as you are, couldn't figure out something like this was bound to happen.

—What could I have done?

—Not left the way you did. Explained it to me, at least.

—Why did you come with the "Melancholy Thug"?

—Who?

—That's what they call Máximo.

—I've never heard that.

—That's what Carmen calls him, at least. I think she got it from a Roberto Arlt novel; he was a character who ran a chain of brothels and wanted to use them to finance a revolution.

—Why did she invite him, then?

—Carmen invites a lot of people, and she and Máximo have always known each other.

—That's what he told me, and he didn't seem particularly happy about it.

—That's why he's the Melancholy Thug.

—He knows Carmen better than you do.

—Don't tell me.

A woman coming out of the bathroom interrupted our conversation as she passed between us.

—I need us to talk, I said.

—It can't be now.

—When?

—Later.

—Later tonight or later like up to now?

—Later, she repeated.

—Have things changed?

—I'm scared, Li replied after a pause.

—Why?

—I'm all alone.

—You're with Carmen, and you could be with me.

—Makes no difference. I'm not alone because of you two.

—But why don't you want to talk?

—I already told you, this isn't the time or place. Don't think everything's a bed of roses with Carmen, and just in case, don't think you don't matter to me. I'm trapped because of what's happened, but for now, I have to be here.

—Why?

—I'd lose my only way out.

—What's that?

—I'm not even sure what it is. But I have to be here for now. That's the only thing I can tell you.

Glenda had appeared in the hall.

—Have you met Glenda? Li inquired.

—No.

—She works at the restaurant.

—How do you do, said Glenda, greeting me. So I finally get to meet you. You're Li's friend. Delighted.

—Likewise.

—Li, said Glenda, Carmen's calling you.

—When can we talk, then? I asked.

—I don't know, but I promise we will. I can't right now.

—Wait, if Noreña is the Melancholy Thug, who am I?

—The Man Who Stares at the Ground as He Walks. He has his charms, believe me. Just like the Melancholy Thug.

Between the living room and the kitchen there were about twenty people. Most were from the university—administrators, professors, and a few students who had come to the party, together with their partners. I knew almost all of them but didn't have a real relationship with practically any. Seeing me in a corner of the living room trying to eavesdrop on the closest conversation and figure out how join in, Noreña came over and took me to the bar they had set up in the kitchen.

—Did it go well? he asked.

—If nothing else, I made contact again. We'll talk later. Apparently it can't be done in the enemy's house.

—Carmen isn't exactly thrilled with your being here. Naturally, I didn't tell her that you might as easily have come without me. I don't know what there is between you, but I'd tell Li she shouldn't trust Carmen.

—Why not?

—Look around you. Probably everybody here felt forced to come. Carmen is a schemer, and she knows how to get what she wants. Sacrificing these hours is preferable to having her as an enemy. That's why we're here. Now she's leaving, and the party is a going-away celebration she organized for herself since she got a job at the university whose name she keeps repeating ad nauseam to astonish us. But I know her very well; at the same time she's frightened about being far away, outside her circle. She needs a companion—much better if she's young and good looking. That is, no doubt, the spot your friend will be filling.

—Why are you telling me this?

—If you want, I'll stop.

—That's not what I mean. What's it to you?

—Let's say, I don't want you to be fooling yourself. Li isn't stupid. She has to be after something, too.

When she saw us standing apart from the others, Carmen Lindo crossed the living room with a wine glass in hand. Her smile could not disguise her unease. She must have been about fifty five, though with her slender build she looked younger.

—Are you having a good time? she asked, turning to me.

—A great time.

—I'm so happy. I assure you, there's no bad blood on my part.

—Nothing less could be expected from you, said Noreña.

—Máximo, this isn't the time, and you haven't made me laugh in twenty years. Anyway, she said after a pause, enjoy yourself as much as you can. Here's Juan Rafael; I'd like you both to talk with him.

The novelist was sitting by one of the doors to the balcony and roaring with laughter. He was dressed in linen trousers and jacket and wore a silk cravat around his neck. You could tell that he had taken advantage of his stay in the tropics to go to the beach.

—He came in the full dress uniform, said Noreña. Don't trust anyone who dresses like that. I bet you anything he's wearing loafers with no socks.

—Juan Rafael, these are some friends, said Carmen. They are excellent Puerto Rican writers.

—I wish you would just call us writers, noted Noreña, looking at the novelist's feet and smiling.

—*Hombre*, anyone would think they were from Navarra! García Pardo exclaimed.

—I also meant the part about being excellent, Noreña clarified.

García Pardo had stood up to embrace us. He paused for an instant to look directly into my eyes. Presumably this combination of gestures constituted a magnanimous greeting.

—They couldn't be at your presentation, Carmen explained, unnecessarily; I, at any rate, never had any intention of going to the event organized by his publisher's San Juan office. But here they are now. Juan Rafael is very interested in Puerto Rican literature, Carmen added for our benefit.

—I had the pleasure of meeting several of your colleagues in Spain, he explained, and on this trip, I shared laughs again with those friends, who are doing as well as always.

—Yes, as always, Noreña cryptically remarked.

—There is so much talent on this island. Gonzalo, my editor, has informed me that Puerto Rico imports a great number of Spanish books. That is surprising when one takes the size of the country into account. It says a good deal about this culture.

—Señor García Pardo, you may not have noticed, I began to say.

—Please, you can call me Juan Rafael.

—Juan Rafael, maybe you haven't noticed, but we're just as Spanish speaking as any other Latin American country.

—But this isn't a country. Not an independent one.

—Which doesn't mean that we're any less Spanish speaking than Spain itself. Besides, the influence of English in the Spanish Caribbean has been a historical constant that purists have often slighted or ignored. Puerto Rico is, in this instance, merely the extreme case in the Greater Antilles.

—Even so, coming from far away, it surprises one. In Spain, we always think of Argentina, of Mexico, of any of the other large countries, but never of Puerto Rico.

—Because we aren't seen. It's like people who go to Barcelona and are surprised that they speak Catalan there.

—Right, but what surprised me was that you import more books than many other Latin American countries with much larger populations.

—We're a country with a passion for consumerism, said

Noreña, with an irony that García Pardo couldn't be entirely sure of.

—The important thing is that we all form part of a common milieu. The Hispanic world unites us all. You have no idea how at home I feel, as much in Mexico City as in San Juan.

—Time is wearing away at that superstition, said Noreña.

—Which?

—The one about a common milieu. The one about the great, common Hispanic world.

—What people have in common looks completely different depending on where you stand, I joined in. Spaniards can't ignore the bigger countries, but they can skip right past all of Central America and a good part of the Caribbean and reduce the rest of Latin America to a handful of images.

—In Spain, we're well informed about Latin America, said García Pardo.

—Do they know anything about Puerto Rico? Many of them think it's a state in the United States, and they think that what you people call the Cuban War had nothing to do with us.

—Well, yours is a bit of a special case.

—Do you know anything about Ecuador, about Guatemala, about Paraguay, other than that they have Indians and dictators?

—But the basis for contact exists, García Pardo explained. Factors favoring unity exist: the language, the common history . . .

—That precisely is the basis of the superstition, said Máximo.

—I don't follow, said García Pardo.

—They overestimate their position and therefore their historical importance.

—*Hombre*, it's hard to ignore Spain!

—But it's very easy to ignore others, Máximo explained, declaring them null from the start, from birth to death, from generation to generation, justifying *everything* by citing a common history of unquestionable values. Within the common tradition you mention, of which I supposedly form a part, I've never seen myself, nor has anyone else seen me.

—Your finest works are published in Spain.

—Works from other Latin American countries, you mean.

—Have it your way, said García Pardo, but countless Latin American writers seek to have their books published in Spain.

—The economic crisis in Latin America has affected their publishing houses, I said. Spain has benefited, but the literature produced by Spaniards themselves is very uneven.

—*Hombre*, there's a bit of everything, García Pardo pointed out. However, there is a whole cohort of important authors now, with complete bodies of work, with translations into several languages.

—And plenty of third-rate literature, Noreña interrupted.

—Which you'll find anywhere, García Pardo retorted.

—But in Spain, it gets published by the bushel. You get tired of reading the same book over and over again.

—What do you mean by that?

—The publishers resort to the same formulas, Noreña explained. And they only have two or three: lots of foreign literature, which is their most substantial contribution, if it weren't so often so badly translated; then books by the usual suspects, or their substitutes from the new generation, with variations on the same offerings.

—Although much of what you say is true, I don't think the case is as devastating as it seems to you.

—This situation is literature's worst enemy, and you Spaniards are on the front lines, Noreña explained.

—It's not so awful. I don't think you're being fair.

—It isn't about being fair, and anyway, literature has never pretended to be; it's not a civil code or a democratic regime. The reader also inhabits a geography, which creates a politics of passions. Literature is still one of the few arenas where it is possible to practice an elegant and constructive terrorism.

—The time of politically committed literature is long gone.

—That's not what I'm talking about at all, Noreña hastened to clarify.

—The novel is free from that burden. Fortunately, people read now for other reasons, García Pardo explained. In a sense, that makes it harder for the writer, who is no longer read simply because he is in political communion with his reader. Now tastes are broader and by the same token more diffuse and demanding. Those are new challenges.

—In other words, we're all victims of the laws of the marketplace, concluded Máximo.

—Of course, García Pardo replied. It's inevitable. We don't like to admit it, but that's the way it is. Writers compete with television, cinema, video games. We can't deceive ourselves.

—A centuries-long dream from which we have awaked into a nightmare, I said.

—Perhaps just so, said the Spaniard. But one must consider that living a dream was not helping us, either. We were all deceiving ourselves.

—But look, I said, you can hardly keep your eyes open reading most books. Spanish literature seems poor. It isn't captivating.

—*Hombre*, captivating, truly captivating work, hardly anyone is doing that anywhere.

—But Spain has high aspirations, I added.

—I don't know what gets over here to you, said García Pardo.

—The same books you have at the Casa del Libro, Noreña put in.

—You should bear in mind, I said, that here we get books imported from many countries. Apart from Spanish publications, we have books from Latin America and full access to the English-language press, aside from what is published inside Puerto Rico. This affords us a perspective that isn't limited by a single culture or a single language.

—I don't think you're up on the current situation. Today's Spain isn't the Spain of Valle-Inclán.

A group of guests had congregated around us, attracted by the tone the debate was taking on. García Pardo's last sentence had produced, because of the tone in which it was said, a bit of alarm. Carmen and Li were watching us with growing concern, fearing that our conversation with the Spaniard might be standing in for talks we weren't having with them, which would have had little to do with literature. Someone had taken our glasses and gone to refill them. The rector of the university was watching from his armchair with the resignation of a man who was, yet again, witnessing a problem arise.

—Come on, let's clear this up. Why are you here in San Juan? Máximo Noreña suddenly asked.

—I came to present *The Angels of Montera Street*, my latest novel.

—But how did you get here? In other words, who organized your trip?

—My publisher, who has a branch here, and also the Book Office at the Spanish Ministry of Culture.

—That is, nobody invited you, Noreña concluded.

—*Hombre*, if you put it that way.

—Don't misinterpret me; what I'm getting at is a question of facts. I'm trying to show that there was no group of readers fascinated by the works of an exemplar of current Spanish literature. It wasn't even a university or a cultural institution that brought you here. They don't have any direct connection with your presence here. Your trip was paid for by a corporation with assistance from a ministry that invests in publicizing Spanish culture around the world.

—Is there anything wrong with that? asked García Pardo.

—That is a matter we could explore later, answered Noreña. My point is, this same advertising structure is what asserts that the great common Hispanic culture of which you speak should be taken to mean the Iberian Peninsula and a few select countries in the Americas. This same structure is what asserts that the biggest selling book is the best.

—You fellows could work with my publisher if you wish. Some Puerto Rican writers have done so.

—That isn't the point of my reflection, Noreña cut him off. What I want to show is how the reputation of a literature gets inflated. Publishing in Spain means nothing and guarantees nothing. It has even come to be a smoke screen. If it meant something during the final years of the Franco dictatorship and the early years of democracy, now it does not have even remotely the same value.

—There's nothing I can do regarding that. It's natural for me to publish my books in my own country.

—But you're part of that framework. What's more, let me tell you, and I'm well aware that I'm being polemical, the worst thing that happened to Spanish literature was when the Franco dictatorship ended.

—*Hombre*, how can you say such a thing! That's such a platitude, it's ridiculous, García Pardo exclaimed in annoyance.

From the way I had observed Noreña closing in on García Pardo, I knew that the result of this exchange would be a mood of dismal gloom. What he said made the border line surrounding us that much darker, separating our words still more from the rest of the world. It was so easy for the Spaniard to dismiss us. Máximo's passion was handing it to him on a silver tray, yet at the same time, I understood perfectly well why he insisted on doing it, why he couldn't say anything else. Centuries of belittlement animated Noreña.

—When Franco died and democracy was established, he explained, Spanish literature couldn't continue justifying its defects and could no longer keep on overvaluing its writers on the basis of their politics. Almost overnight, protest songs vanished. Since that time, the writers under democracy haven't had a mantle to protect them and have even proved themselves inferior to the postwar writers. In one generation, faced with the conceptual vacuum created by the end of the Franco years, Spanish literature has done nothing but flounder and show this allegedly common culture its uselessness.

—I see where you're coming from, but I cannot agree. Spain has produced a century of great literature, before, during, and after Franco.

—It's been an insular literature that doesn't resonate beyond the peninsula.

—And where would you leave Unamuno, the Generation of '27, and Lorca?

—I'll give you the first one, Noreña said. Unamuno was one the last intellectuals to confront his own society, and that always has some force. The Generation of '27, apart from Lorca, was a local phenomenon, and his influence extended only to Latin America and in a very temporary way. Postwar Spain clung to them and mythified them, making them much more than a literary phenomenon.

—It's the same with you, said García Pardo.

—With who? asked Noreña.

—All you, the Latin Americans.

—To a certain degree you're right. For a long time, Latin America was a poor copy of Spain. But this part of the world is where literature in Spanish was revived.

—That claim has to be approached with a critical eye, too, García Pardo responded. The Boom was invented by a Catalan publisher, and years ago, García Márquez ceased to be the towering figure he had become. Cortázar, it's a shame to say it, but now he looks like a writer for little love-struck couples, and Borges is an Argentine show-off.

—Those are rather simplistic opinions, I said.

—Like yours, García Pardo replied.

—We were talking about Spain anyway, said Noreña.

Carmen had set a fresh glass of whiskey on the table for García Pardo, who took advantage of the pause to light a cigarette.

—I detect tremendous frustration in you fellows, said García Pardo. Puerto Rico is a small country and that perhaps has something to do with it. You gain nothing by taking it out on us. We aren't your enemies. I'm not even sure if enemies exist.

—You're wrong, said Noreña.

—Mind telling me why? said García Pardo, who was starting to look for a way to end the conversation.

—Literature can't bear a sham. That is what I am talking about. Today, Spain doesn't have a literature; it has a publishing industry, and good readers hate being sold a bill of goods. I don't question the value of some authors, but they're victims of the industry, too.

—Oh, God! That's all we need!

—A literature, Noreña went on, is more than a pile of books. A literature, no matter how minor and limited it is, such as Puerto Rican literature or the literatures of other countries around Latin America and the world, cannot be confined to being an endless succession of books. It has to grapple with something. Now, I'm confronting you and the world you come from. Tomorrow, it will be something else. The best of Spanish literature was what came from the writers who were, so to speak, anti-Spanish, external and internal exiles who couldn't be at peace with the brutalization of their society. Today, they're nearly an extinct species.

—Máximo, said García Pardo, that won't get you anywhere. Only to hatred. Excuse me.

García Pardo stood up and left the living room. The guests surrounding us opened up to let him leave, and we all remained silent.

—Enough already, said Carmen. Juan Rafael is in my house, and this isn't the treatment he deserves.

—And what sort should he have been given? I asked.

Carmen looked at me for an instant, wheeled about turning her back on me, and walked off in search of the writer. Li, who had been present at the debate, approached me.

—I hope what you said had nothing to do with me, she said.

—You know it didn't, though now that you mention it, I think it did, that it had a lot to do with you. Anyway, I wasn't the lead singer.

—You were a duo.

—You look different. You even sound different.

—So do you.

—Is your friend going to let you see me?

—The situation is complicated. I lost my job and lots of things have happened since the last night. I'm sorry for getting you mixed up in my problems, but it couldn't have been otherwise.

—You're moving away? I asked. That's what I heard.

—I don't know yet, but probably.

—In other words, that's your way out.

Li did not answer; she took my hand, and we embraced.

—I'll call you and we'll see each other. I promise you. You'd better go before they throw you out, she said, smiling.

We could hear voices from the other rooms. García Pardo, Carmen, and somebody else were talking very loudly. I went out the front door without saying good-bye to anyone. Noreña was waiting for me by the stairs.

—Cigarette? he offered.

It was back to smoking.

Rumors soon circulated about the scandal into which the debate with García Pardo had devolved. Carmen Lindo's rage had been monumental. For the rest of the soirée and over the next few days, she had probably not talked about anything else. My having shown up uninvited, my having been Li's partner and Noreña's friend, together with our bitter debate with the Spaniard, gave Carmen an open invitation to slander me. When I went by La Tertulia one afternoon, I felt too many eyes staring at my back. A few of the people who worked there, being more informed than anyone else regarding tales great and small from the literary world, stopped me to ask about the affair. I learned through them that the prevailing version accused us, Noreña and me, of being arrogant and envious.

The controversy had served to air some old dissatisfactions. Noreña and I came out of it as a couple of minor hacks with outsized egos who had gone after the foreign writer with fever-crazed arguments. We were accused of being chauvinists, and countless professors of language and literature imputed a new mental illness to us: Hispanophobia. A novelist who, for other reasons, had earlier tried to tear us both to pieces saw the confrontation as the shameful proof of our Frenchification. Few sympathized with our position, and even fewer among them understood what had brought it about. In the end, Carmen made her move and, to mollify the great author, got the Department of Hispanic Studies to hold a discussion session with him in the university auditorium.

I called Máximo, who had given me his phone number when we said good-bye that night, and found that he already knew all about it. He told me to meet him the following day on the foot bridge connecting Muñoz Rivera Park and Escambrón Beach. I arrived early and strolled up and down the tree-lined walks. I liked feeling the gravel of that park beneath my feet, looking at the cement benches built to look like tree branches, some of them almost a century old. Not a soul was there, naturally enough, on a workday afternoon.

At the agreed-upon time, I found Noreña watching the traffic from the center of the bridge. We went and sat facing the sea on the stairs next to what was once the Naval Reserve Officers' Club.

—You haven't seen Li? he asked.

—Not yet, I replied.

—You may have to wait a while. García Pardo is leaving today.

—We're really getting dumped on.

—By the same people as always. I'm used to it. Still, they're right about one thing. I spoke, maybe so did you, with all the harshness of someone who no longer expects anything. Not even a gesture of friendship. It's the voice of disillusionment and the open wound, a voice that leaves no room for anyone. I believe in what I said, I think it is regrettably true, but I didn't allow García Pardo to see that perhaps he, too, is a victim.

—It seems to me, I said, that he wouldn't have been willing to entertain the idea. He's fully accepted his function as the writer on the autograph tour. From his point of view, he's made it, and we don't figure in the game. He was probably expecting us to ask him to sign a copy of his book and banter with him about banalities. He never imagined we'd start questioning the ground he stands on.

—That ground, or so it seems to me, is what a writer must mistrust the most. That was what I was trying to express. There in Spain, they've lost their way. They have a literary scene that requires manuscripts, whole reams for each and every season. A novelist is nothing but a producer churning out stories, a professional narrative-maker. There's nothing that rubs the wrong way because almost all books do one thing: endeavor to make time melt away in the reader's hands. That is the impoverishment I was speaking of. At this extreme, literature as we understand it is dead, or it survives almost underground, pushed farther and farther each day from the new arrivals table. Here, as in other countries where the literary marketplace barely exists, there still endures a type of writer that has been slowly disappearing in societies where publishing has become almost exclusively a business. Frailty in the culture of letters is always the manifestation of a despicable time, a brutal and naïve era.

—The funny thing, I said, is that there are lots of publishers in Spain that only publish translations. Their doubts about, if not outright disdain for, their own nation's writers is plain enough right there. What's surprising is that writers only complain about it in private, they don't write about the subject. It's as if they were all hoping to sneak onto the list, dreaming of the day when they'll get the chance to be the exception.

—The problem is that they are so alone, said Noreña. As alone as we are, but they don't realize it because they move in circles where there are real reputations and, sometimes, lots of money. You have to be brave not to join the charade. The risks are high. There isn't much that one writer can do against a publishing world that starts to perceive him as a content provider. The record industry killed music. The book industry is in the process of annihilating literature. We're castaways; all we have left is the bitter future of those who've survived from a world that will never exist again. What we wanted to do in our lifetimes no longer exists.

Noreña fell silent and for a few seconds we watched the sea.

—But I can't live without that mirage, he went on. That's why I was so adamant with García Pardo. He's an impostor. A little talent and a lot of favorable circumstances. His books are dead after six months. He'll never become a tragic figure because he had opportunities and knew how to use them.

—We're bound to the day when a book bedazzled us, I said.

—Very likely so. That's why, in spite of it all, we turned into writers. A few days ago, I told a young man not to become a writer if he could help it. It takes years to be convinced that it's practically a life sentence. Yes, the first book that bedazzled us. We want to recreate as closely as we can the force that shocked us on that day. To bring it back to life, but through our own efforts this time, using the stuff of our own lives. García Pardo probably experienced this, too, but he opted for eight hours a day in front of a keyboard, like any office drone.

We sat in silence, smoking the small cigars.

—We're alone, so alone.

I watched as the smoke carried his words away.

—I sent you an e-mail, he said. Have you seen it?

When I got home, I went straight to the computer and read the message that for some mysterious reason Máximo decided to write and send just before we met.

"Carmen is leaving for California. García Pardo has come to visit. Two movements, very much alike in their own way to one who has decided to remain here. Carmen is going where she can breathe deeply from a different atmosphere, construct her personal happiness, and who knows whether she will ever want to return. García Pardo is traveling through 'the provinces' and will return to Madrid convinced that, despite it all, he is in the best of all possible places. What happens when you wish to honor these streets not because they deserve any special tribute but because almost your whole past took place here, because here is what made us yearn to set it to paper? None of these questions have answers. You can't even assess these things or formulate an idea that's close to correct. We're left with a pain we cannot relieve, a pain we feel each time someone walks by without seeing us, blinded by his tinseled traditions. Peace is impossible and that is perhaps why we write, and since writing does not relieve that pain either, writing becomes an obsessive, pointless act. It's just another sentence, another paragraph, another page, and we can never finish. Best case, someone reads something we write and finds it unforgettable. We've all had such experiences ourselves, and they have marked us, but there are already too many unforgettable texts in the world.

"What is taken for success in literature matters less and less to me each day, even if I can't help seeking it. I know now that it won't solve anything, that at most it will cool the pain and make me write less willingly, and I will more closely resemble García Pardo and so many like him. I know I can only live by repeating a gesture that separates me from most of humanity. And without really knowing why, I feel that it is very important for me to wear myself out doing it. Out of choice or out of necessity.

"When we live like this, let this attitude determine our lives, the choice between staying or emigrating no longer has any meaning. We're always alone, irremediably alone, with our rage. The rage of the place and the life we were fated to have. And then, sitting before a blank page some day or some night, you realize that this, precisely, is the point, that you had to get to the end of the dead-end street to be able to set something down on paper that's worth the trouble. Worth the pain. That's when you know: this is writing. A writer is an athlete of defeat. All the rest is *not* literature. That is García Pardo's problem (and his tragedy)."

Frailty. All the times I've been weak, the times I've collapsed. To remember those times in order to know what it really means to live here. Here, I am fragile as I am nowhere else. My fault lines and fissures are here.

Happiness is bound up with coming back home. I was hoping for Li. I was hoping for happiness. I was hoping for the impossible, and therefore I kept on hoping and waiting. I was tied to what I had lost, and over these days, the yearning I felt for her could only be compared to what I had gone through when I was getting her messages, when I feared, each moment, that I was about to lose someone I still hadn't found. The situation now was similar, but there was a scent of decay. Who was it that had been here and had gone? Was it really the woman with whom I had shared days and nights, or was it, sadly, the absurd absence of a body in which I had believed with a faith that was blind?

I was immersed in thought, unaware of my surroundings. Seconds passed, maybe a minute or more. That was it: the drawing Li had left in the mailbox on the day she had asked me to meet at the Cine Paradise. I searched for it. I had put it away in a drawer with all the others. I didn't need to look at it to know, but I felt an urge to check and be certain. It was half a sheet torn from a drawing notebook, with a rectangle in black ink. It had attracted my attention at first because it was less dense than the others, allowing minute patches of paper to show through. It was my name. It had been made by writing and crossing out my name hundreds of times within a restricted space. It was her attempt to say what she already knew. The rest had been fear, exhaustion, a horrible good-bye. Li had given herself to me knowing she could not stay, knowing that the moment she made love to me she would have to leave.

She wouldn't come to see me, or she would come too late to tell me what she already knew. There would be no good-bye, and I knew that she wouldn't think it wrong. Someday, I'd hear about her, when we no longer counted for each other.

I went back to the living room, got a sheet of paper, and in one go wrote down a poem that had been brewing for weeks:

Take refuge in the multiplied unknown
Always this voice   this voice whose voice?
which writes when there is no one here
    when to be is not a verb
Stay here in this nook   this nothing site
forget the forgetting of remembrance
write on this page indifferent to you
write with no desire to write   that is   not really
with this absurd absence of your body

Then, a little later, came sleep, my exhaustion a narcotic. I slept for many hours, and opening my eyes when day had already come, a tremendous weight still kept me glued onto the sheets.

At last I got up, thirsty and needing the bathroom. The silence on that morning was different. It was spongy and slowed my movements down. There was something familiar about it. It was what I had lived before Li. I found out then that hope would now produce only shame.

Máximo called around midday.

—I have two pieces of news for you, he said. Both bad.

—I guess it doesn't matter much which you tell me first.

—García Pardo just won a major award in Madrid. The Grand Asshole of Letters or some such.

—We're screwed.

—Seriously.

—What's the second?

—Carmen Lindo leaves tomorrow. I suppose Li goes too.

—Thanks for the report.

—Did you care for her?

—Why the past tense? Who, Li?

—Yes.

—I thought, though it makes me look like the biggest idiot in the world, that it might work out. But we all delude ourselves.

—That's the way it is, said Noreña. Look at the panel of judges in Madrid.

—But I don't gain anything by being deluded.

—Neither does García Pardo.

I had to guess what the sound was because even though I'd been home since early in the morning I had kept all the windows closed. It sounded like someone knocking on the locked front gate. Seconds later, a car honked. Stealthily I went to peer from behind the curtain in the living room. Li was looking toward the house, toward the window behind which I was hiding, striving to find some sign of my presence. Behind her, Glenda honked the car horn again. Probably the same car she had borrowed from her cousin the day we first met.

I waited, holding my breath. There was the woman I loved, but I would not open the door. I waited until she looked at Glenda without saying a word. Glenda honked the horn again and Li shouted my name, once, twice, three times. I watched her face flush with emotion and closed my eyes. When I opened them, I saw her get into the car and return with a notebook. She looked for a page, tore it out, and put it in the mailbox. She looked at the house one last time, shouted my name louder than all the times before, and Glenda leaned on the horn. Then, burying her face in her hands, the same gesture as when she had cried for such a long time in my living room, she got into the car, and her friend stepped on the accelerator.

When the sound of the engine had disappeared into the distance, I unplugged the telephone. Hours later, when it was already night, I opened the door stealthily and found the sheet of paper. It was the first time Li had written me more than a couple of lines:

"All my life I have suffered from bending to authority. I have spent my life on the lookout for someone whom I do not know but who always says no. I have preferred solitude—I have learned everything I know by myself, even at the university, where I had no advisers or genuine teachers (Carmen, in reality, was not one)—in a fruitless attempt to escape from a power that was all too real for me.

"I have only had this barren space. Hence my readiness to make do with scarcity and privation.

"I have not been in the habit of living among equals. My lesbianism is in a way an ironic statement. It is very likely I have never known this situation, that of being on the same level as another person. I have inhabited the margins without being free.

"You will never read this, but this is my attempt to apologize."

On reaching the last line, I finally knew why Li had chosen me. I was her match, one half of an impossible couple, half of two bodies that had never met their mates in any other. Something, at the outset of our lives, had conveyed to us the great *no*.

I folded the torn sheet in four and sat in the dark living room, in the same place where I had spent so many nights with her, and I recognized, finally, what my life entailed, why it was like this, why it could not have been otherwise. I was unable to move a muscle or speak a word. An enormous unremitting wave racked my body from head to foot. It was the accumulated weight of all the years I had lived. Once more, I would not undertake any action. No phone call, no stormy visit to Calle Canals. I would stay here. My cry for help was silence and stillness.

That night I went outside and in thick wax crayon wrote "This absurd absence of your body" over walls and sidewalks. For hours and hours, I scrawled the conclusion—a kind of mourning for an unending loss. What was left was the city, the turf where I still belonged, despite it all. I inscribed its surfaces with my naked grief, tormented, one moment on the verge of tears, the next seething with anger. I'd never be able to leave this city, after walking its streets like this, without shame, turning them into a page for me to write on. My agony bound me to them forever. My naked feelings told me, these streets were my fate.